# Cyclone

## Savage Brotherhood MC: Book Seven

## A Paranormal Romance

by Jasmine Wylder

## Table of Contents

# Chapter One

*Stewart*

The worst part about being the only non-shifter of three siblings was that he'd spent his whole life being looked after. Sure, maybe there was benefit to it from time to time. Stewart wasn't a kid anymore, though, and his older brother and sister tended to overlook that fact. They thought he needed protecting from everything in the world. Every time he sneezed, it seemed like they were there, hovering with a box of tissues and advice to drink plenty of fluids and get plenty of rest.

Stewart loved his siblings. After their parents were brutally murdered by vampires, they were all he had. But that didn't mean he needed to be watched after every second of the day!

He could remember the anticipation he'd felt when he was young and watched them shift into their wolf forms. It wasn't always the case that a child would turn into the same sort of animal as their parents, but in the case of Roxy and Andy, they had. He'd been so excited to join them... the excitement turned to worry as years passed and still nothing, and eventually anger, then the reluctant acceptance of what he was.

Human.

"That'll be five sixty-eight," he told the customer at his till.

The little old lady shelled out the cash for the present for her grandson and, thanking him profusely, tottered off. Stewart sighed as he moved out from behind the counter to resume sweeping up the little second-hand shop he ran. It wasn't protecting people from the threat of vampires, but it was better than nothing. He could at least use the storefront as a way for the Savage Brotherhood, a motorcycle club full of shifters, of which Andy was a member, to move some of their cash assets around. He wasn't allowed to be a full-on member, as humans were far too weak to participate in the dangers of the gang, but it was something, at least.

He'd almost given up on his dream to one day be a shifter. There was a method to turn humans into shifters, including a ritual and a full-on shifter biting the human. The last time he'd tried it, though, he'd been badly injured and not a single strand of fur had appeared.

Since then, Andy had refused to try again. *It's too dangerous*, he said. *It's better you live as a human than die as a shifter.*

Stewart grunted as he kicked aside a pile of cloth that a previous customer had left on the floor, then bent to fold it up. *Are you going to be saying that when I'm on my human deathbed? Shifters live longer than humans.*

At least, they did naturally. They also healed faster, were stronger, had finer-turned senses. All in all, being a shifter was heads-and-shoulders above being a human. Roxy and Andy didn't understand what it was like, to be so weak and helpless all the time... they'd never gotten so much as a cold in their lives!

His cellphone buzzed in his pocket. Stewart set the broom aside and fished the phone from his pocket. His dour mood lifted when he saw who it was calling.

He answered it with a grin on his face. “Polaris. Fancy hearing from you.”

“Don’t be a smartass,” Frieda’s cheerful voice came over the line. “It’s getting to be time for you to close up shop, right?”

“Yup.” He glanced at the clock. “Fifteen more minutes.”

“Good. I’m in the neighborhood. I’ll stop by and help you clean up. Then I thought we could go grab a movie or something. It’s been awfully boring lately… the cops keep sticking their noses where they don’t belong, so Typhoon has called for laying low for a bit. No jobs, no missions, not even going after vamps! I’m going stir-crazy with nothing to do.”

Stewart smiled wryly. Oh, if only she knew what true boredom was. She at least had the luxury of impatiently waiting for the next mission, the next vampire attack. But Frieda was his best friend. They'd known each other for years now, ever since she'd joined Andy's crew. These days, she'd been promoted to leading her own crew, many of whom used to run with Andy before he married Guinevere, a vampire queen, and became an official ambassador.

It had taken some getting used to, having a vampire sister-in-law. Guinevere was good people, though, not like the vampires who killed wantonly. They'd even figured out the secret to having vampire-shifter hybrid children. Stewart wasn't sure if they were going to have more children, but they already had a boy, Daniel.

"Yo, Stewie. You there?" Frieda barked over the phone.

"Yeah, I'm here." Stewart shook off his thoughts. "Movie sounds great. There's a new horror out, right?"

"Yup. That's exactly what I was thinking."

Stewart smiled. "See you soon, then."

When he hung up, he glanced around the shop. It had been a pretty dead day, and there wasn't much left to do. If he worked quickly and was blessed with no more customers, then it was a fair bet that he'd be ready to go by the time Frieda arrived. He might even be able to wheedle some information out of her about what the gang was up to.

The thought of spending time with her brightened his day considerably. His stomach actually started to twist into knots. Perhaps this would be the day when he told her. They'd been best friends for years, and he wanted more than friendship between them. He wasn't ashamed to admit that there had been nights, when he was kept awake by thoughts of his humanity, where he imagined her in his bed. Those were always his favorite fantasies.

But he knew it wasn't going to happen. Frieda had said on more than one occasion that shifter-human relationships didn't work out. Humans were too frail. He didn't know if she sensed his feelings for her and was trying to gently discourage them or they were just off-the-cuff remarks, but the effect was the same.

Besides, it would be super weird for Andy. Him and Frieda were like siblings, and for Stewart and Frieda to become a couple? Stewart shook his head, chuckling at the mental image of Andy's face should that come to light.

The bell over the door jangled. Stewart scowled as he turned, though he quickly put on the Customer Service Smile (patent pending). "Hi, we're actually closing early to…"

Stewart's voice died away when the man who entered pointed a gun at him. The man was tall, thin, with sunken eyes. He wore a dirty coat, ragged pants and looked quite rough overall. There was an angry gleam in his eye, though, one that Stewart had never seen in the random people who had tried to rob him in the past. Slowly, he lifted his hands into the air.

"Easy, there," he started, keeping his voice low and soothing. "Cash register is already open, go ahead and take what you want."

"Oh, I will." The man stalked forward and aimed the gun at Stewart's forehead. "I am going to take exactly what I want. Your life."

Even before the man finished speaking, Stewart had kicked the broomstick up. He caught it in his hands while dodging to one side. The gun went off, the crack and whistle ringing in his ears. He twisted, swinging the broom out; it hit the man in the face, and Stewart brought it down on the man's hand with a crack. The gun went off again, the bullet narrowly missing Stewart's foot. He dodge in closer, punching the man in the face while he grabbed the gun and twisted it out of his hand, the way Andy had taught him.

The man staggered back, hissing. Stewart's eyes widened as a set of long, white fangs slipped into view. A vampire? Attacking him? Not only in the heart of Ivywood, but in broad daylight as well? He brought the gun up and pressed it to the vampire's chest, emptying the clip rapidly.

The vampire dropped. He grunted, drops of blackened blood dripping from the wounds on his chest while one hand grabbed a nearby shelf, trying to keep himself upright. Stewart didn't take any chances; lifting the broom again, he gave the vampire a mighty whack over the head. This time, he collapsed to the floor and stayed down.

Stewart stared at him for a moment, his heart pounding. He glanced around, then strode over to the metal bat that he'd recently purchased. Downed or not, vampires were too dangerous to let alone. Frieda would be here soon, and he had to make sure this vampire wasn't going to be causing trouble for him before then.

As he turned back to smash the vampire's head in, though, he came face-to-face with another man. A wide grin on this man's face already showed the pearly-white fangs. Stewart let out a strangled shout as the vampire punched him hard in the stomach. He bent double, the air rushing from his lungs. The vampire lifted him bodily and tossed him across the room, several shelves' worth of valuables collapsing over him as Stewart fell to the floor.

Dazed, Stewart tried to push himself to his feet. His head spun, and he fell back to one knee.

"What do you want?" Stewart spat out, trying to buy himself some time. Pain lanced up his spine, making him feel shaky. He gripped the metal bat tightly in one hand, even though he was fairly certain what these vampires were after.

And sure enough, when the vampire spoke, his suspicions were confirmed. "To make the queen's filthy mate understand what it means to interfere in vampire business."

"You realize I had nothing to do with my brother marrying Guinevere, right?"

The vampire didn't respond. He only lunged for Stewart. Stewart grunted, rolling out of the way of the vampire's long claws. He whipped the bat around, hitting the vampire square in the face. The vampire's head was knocked back, a satisfying crunch indicating that his nose was broken. As he clutched his face, Stewart took the opportunity to get to his feet. He swung the bat hard. This time the vampire was too quick.

"Fight all you want," the vampire seethed as he bounced to his feet. "I enjoy the challenge! It would be too easy otherwise. I am going to rend you limb from limb. I will take you apart and suck you dry of blood. Then I will send your severed head to your brother. What do you say to that?"

Stewart grunted as he swung the bat again. It smacked into the vampire's shoulder, but the vampire grabbed it with his free hand. He yanked hard, dragging Stewart towards him. Stewart dropped, kicking the vampire's legs apart. The vampire didn't seem to mind, though; he dropped over Stewart, grabbing his wrists and pinned him to the floor.

His fangs flashed as the vampire bent his head toward Stewart's neck...

And in the next second, the vampire had been ripped away. Stewart gasped in relief as Frieda's familiar grey wolf dragged the vampire back from him. She threw him over her shoulder. As the vampire twisted in mid-air and landed in a crouched position on the floor, Frieda was already going after him again.

It didn't last long. Frieda methodically ripped the vampire apart, until it was a bloody mess on the floor. Stewart quickly moved to the windows and drew the shades, even though in this neighborhood it was unlikely that many people cared about what was going on in his store. The place was a freaking mess, though… it was going to take days to clean it up!

Frieda shifted back to her human form, and Stewart silently yanked a sheet from a nearby stack of bedding to hand to her. Not that he minded the brief glimpses of her body that he was graced with, but, given the situation, the last thing on his mind was ogling his friend.

"You alright?" Frieda asked, cocking a brow at him.

His left leg was trembling with effort to keep himself upright and his whole body was pained, but Stewart nodded. It was nothing he couldn't handle. "There's another vampire over there. I got him with the gun, and since they have to be partly human to go out in sunlight..."

Freida nodded. She put an arm around him and helped him to a chair, which he sank gratefully into, before she went to check on the first vampire. He was a little more beat up than he first thought. His spine ached and his chest hurt when he breathed in. His left leg was bleeding pretty good, too, and there were numerous small cuts on his arms and face that he hadn't realized were there until he had the chance to sit.

"Well, he's dead," Frieda called. She wended her way through the aisles to return to him. “Your first vampire kill. Impressive, if I do say so myself.”

Stewart grunted in annoyance. “Impressive for a human, you mean.”

“Stewie—”

“If I was a shifter, I could have handled both of them.” He scowled at the floor, then yanked his cellphone from his pocket. He pressed it into Freida’s hand. “Call Typhoon. It’s time for this to be over. There have been plenty of threats on my life directly since Andy and Guinevere got together. Unless he wants to waste resources protecting me or just let me die, something’s got to change.”

Frieda glanced at the phone warily. “You know the rules. We’re not allowed to call him directly unless we’re using a phone belonging to the Brotherhood."

"I might as well be a member," Stewart snapped. "I have been involved in Brotherhood business for as long as I can remember. Just because I don't have the tattoo doesn't mean I'm immune to it all. So you call him. Tell him what happened today, and let him know that I'm fed up with all this. If I'm going to be threatened by vampires and dealing with the cops sniffing around and all that, I am not going to be left on the outside anymore."

Frieda studied him for a moment. Her brow furrowed in worry, but she nodded slowly and took the phone. "If killing a vampire doesn't show him that you're strong enough to go through the ritual, I don't know what will be."

Stewart nodded his agreement, although the reminder of the ritual made his stomach twist. All previous attempts to turn him into a shifter had failed. What if it just wasn't in his DNA? What if they went through all the proper channels and had professionals help and it still wouldn't take? What if he was doomed to be human for the rest of his life?

He shifted his position and grimaced as pain shot through him. No. He couldn't think about what might happen if it didn't take—it *had* to take. The problem in the past was it was just him and Andy, without knowing all the proper steps. Once Typhoon and the Brotherhood were involved, it was going to work out. They'd complete the ritual, and he would be a shifter.

He *had* to be.

During all this, Frieda had been speaking quietly on the phone. She nodded once and hung up before turning to Stewart. “Typhoon wants to see you. He’ll be sending people here to clean up for you.”

“Good,” Stewart grunted. “Let’s go.”

## Chapter Two

*Polaris*

Stewart and Typhoon argued with each other for hours, with Stewart not backing down one smidgeon, before Typhoon finally burst into laughter, called him a real Cyclone and agreed to let him attempt to become a shifter. "If that's successful, then I'll see about letting you join the Brotherhood. Not sure why the tattoo is so important to you, though. You've got plenty others."

Frieda traced her own tattoo, the wolf's head that marked her as part of the Brotherhood. She'd had it for, oh, ten years now. Ever since she joined the Brotherhood as a teen. It seemed like a lifetime ago before she had been involved in all this fighting and death and crime. Not that she wanted to go back to the girl she used to be, always terrified, always uncertain. There was a certain loneliness, though, an aching for the brother who always took care of her.

She sighed as she glanced around the room. There was no time for those thoughts today.

The attempt to turn Stewart into a shifter was taking place in Hurricane's country house. It seemed fitting, given that Hurricane was Stewart's brother-in-law and there was a large patch of forest outside, perfect for running in. Not to mention the Brotherhood often used this space as a hideout when things got a little rough. It was charmed against vampire attacks, and Hurricane was rich enough that the cops didn't like to bother him unless they had something big.

Hurricane and Roxy were here, as were Twister, Guinevere, and Daniel. Stewart talked with them quietly, and Frieda dropped her arms to her sides. Given her and Stewart's relationship, it had been decided that she was going to be the one doing the riskiest part of the ritual—the biting. Twister refused to try again, and Stewart had decided not to put Roxy or Hurricane through that. But he wanted someone he trusted, someone who cared, and so Frieda had volunteered herself.

If something went wrong, though...

*It won't,* she told herself firmly. *And if it does, which it won't, then Dr. Mia is here.*

Typhoon's mate stood by him, hands clasped lightly before herself. Her expression was calm and smooth, and she nodded toward Frieda when she saw her looking. Typhoon touched his mate's arm, then strode to the middle of the room, where the candles were already in place and the runes drawn in chalk on the floor.

"Frieda." Typhoon gestured to her.

She repressed a sigh. Frieda. Always her *name*. She knew the gang was largely a boy's club—after all, it was called the Savage *Brother*hood—but it irked her when her chosen nickname wasn't used. It wasn't like she could tell the alpha of the whole gang to shove it, though. Still... she bet that Shadow didn't have this problem, even though she'd semi-retired from the Brotherhood.

*Then again,* Frieda mused as she joined Typhoon in the center of the ritual circle, *Shadow's fucking terrifying. Girl's a berserker along with everything else she's got.*

That utter loss of control was not something that Frieda would take in trade for being called Polaris. She clasped her hands behind her back and nodded to Stewart as he stepped into the circle as well.

"We all know the risks involved in this." Typhoon glanced from one to the other before sweeping his gaze across the others in the room, lingering on Daniel before turning back to Stewart.

Frieda had to wonder what that was about. As the only half-vampire, half-shifter hybrid in existence, Daniel was an interesting case. Looking at him, you'd think he was Andy's slightly younger brother, not his son. The fact was, though, that Typhoon was against Andy and Guinevere's relationship from the start. She could only guess that it meant he was keeping an extra eye on Daniel. It had made her nervous, too, even though she didn't want to admit it. Still, Daniel was a good kid... well... 'kid' was pushing it a bit. In some ways, she wasn't certain he'd been a kid at all.

"Stewart," Typhoon said slowly, a furrow in his brow, "Have you given thought to what you want if this doesn't work?"

"If you mean if I die," Stewart said slowly, "I already have my will written out and final goodbyes put on tape and all that jazz."

Typhoon frowned at him. “I was more thinking along the lines of if it doesn’t work and you’re too close to death to remain human. Have you given thought to Guinevere turning you into a vampire?”

Frieda’s eyes widened. She attempted to stifle her gasp, though it did little good. It was almost as shocking that nobody else seemed surprised at this line of questioning. Stewart didn’t even blink as he nodded.

“I thought about it. Guinevere and I discussed what it means to be a vampire and what the first years are like. I have decided not to pursue that option, if it comes to it.”

*Why would he choose to be a vampire? Even if death was the only other option?* Frieda kept her expression smooth, so that her thoughts couldn't be read on her face. She hadn't spent a lot of time with Guinevere, but one of the things that she did say, over and over again, was how much she missed being human.

It was time for the ritual. Stewart removed his shirt, the tattoos on his chest and shoulders rippling as he did so, and then knelt before her. Frieda swallowed hard, not daring to let herself second-guess this decision now. She pressed a single finger to his forehead; not part of the ritual, just a touch to calm both of their nerves.

Then she shifted. And without letting herself think about the consequences, she snapped her jaws around his neck. Her teeth punctured his jugular as the candles flickered and the runes seemed to glow. Stewart let out a half-strangled cry of pain. Frieda drew back, shifting into her human form, and grabbed the blood transfusion tube on the floor. While she chanted the words she had memorized, she quickly connected herself to the tube, letting the blood flow through it before sticking the other end into Stewart's arm; Mia hovered on the outside, but Frieda didn't look at her. She didn't care if she didn't do it exactly as the tiger had said; this would suffice.

Blood pumped into the air as Stewart clasped a hand to his neck. His eyes rolled into the back of his head as Frieda finished the chant. A ripple of power wafted through the air; not quite electricity, and not quite magic, either. As he collapsed to the floor, his blood staining the wooden floor red, Frieda lunged forward and caught him. Her heart crashed against her ribs again and again as she lowered him gently to the floor.

She didn't need to find his pulse to know that it was all out of order. She could hear his heart, the beat irregular. Her hands started to shake as she bent over him, one hand on his chest.

"Let me," Mia urged, suddenly there beside her.

Frieda allowed the doctor to nudge her aside, though she felt likc snarling, hunching over him, preventing anybody from going near him. Beyond the circle, Twister and Roxy clung to each other while their mates watched with tense shoulders. Daniel's hands were clenched as he bounced slightly on the spot. Typhoon watched with hard eyes that didn't quite conceal his worry.

"Hold him," Mia cried as Stewart started to convulse.

"No," Frieda moaned, throwing herself on Stewart. She pressed his limbs to the floor, taking special care that the tube giving him her blood didn't disconnect. Tears started to fill her eyes, even though she tried to push the awful, empty feeling in her chest away. He wasn't dead yet! "What do I need to do?"

"Just hold him."

Obeying the doctor, Frieda increased her hold on Stewart. His cheeks were pale, the blood flow starting to ease. Mia worked on him, keeping one hand pressed firmly to his neck. His heart stuttered—Frieda nearly cried out. It gave a lurch, was still for far too long, and then started to beat again.

Relief washed over her so powerfully that she was left trembling as she kept holding him, even though his seizing had stopped. His heartbeat was strong and steady now. Mia pulled her hand back, checked his neck, and a smile curved her lips. She wiped the blood from her hands and pulled back Stewart's lip, checking his color, then lifted his eyelid and shone a light into his eye.

"Watch it," he slurred, pulling weakly against Frieda. She let him go and he batted at Mia's hand. "What're you doing, trying to blind me or something?"

Cries of happiness rang from around the room. Mia checked his vitals as Stewart's family crowded together. Mia unhooked the transfusion tube, then nodded at Frieda. She withdrew, standing beyond the circle with her arms wrapped around her waist. He was alive… that was good. Now it only remained to be seen if the ritual worked… if he was a shifter or it had just been her blood to heal him.

"God!" Stewart twisted his head and stared at Guinevere in shock. "You *stink*!"

"Hey." Twister slapped his arm even as he started to laugh.

Frieda grinned. That Stewart was smelling that god-awful rotten fruit scent was a good indication… But she still held her breath.

Until Stewart threw back his head and let out such a deep, rich howl that her wolf responded at once. Heat flooded her body at the sound. Her breath caught in her chest as snow-white fur sprouted across his body. Her eyes widened as his clothes tore from his body. His muscled body shifted shape, and within seconds a white wolf, almost as big as Typhoon's wolf form, stood in the living room.

Frieda couldn't help it. She leapt forward, adding in her howl as she shifted back to her wolf's form. Hurricane hurried to the door and opened it; together, the two of them bounded onto the large manicured lawn. Stewart leapt and rolled and danced in circles. Frieda's tail went in wide circles as she dashed after him. She pounced on his back, nipping at his shoulders, and he quickly turned. With a great roll, he turned her over his shoulder and then pinned her to the grassy yard.

Roxy and Twister bounded over, also in their wolf forms. They circled them, and together the three siblings bounded around, howling in unison and yipping with happiness. Frieda panted as she rolled to her stomach, watching while her tail continued to wag. She had never seen Stewart so happy. Her heart was so full of warmth that she couldn't take it.

This was the first step. He'd gotten what he wanted, but it didn't mean that he was automatically going to get the rest of what he wanted. These first few weeks would be crucial in establishing his control over his wolf. They were powerful beasts and wonderful allies, but they did have a tendency to react to everything in the immediacy. Not much for thinking ahead of circumstances.

After some time, the siblings calmed. They rubbed heads and licked each other's cheeks before trotting back to the porch where Typhoon waited with the rest of them. He had a pleased smirk on his face. Guinevere looked relieved, whereas Daniel had his arms wrapped around his chest and looked like he was struggling to be happy for his uncle.

Frieda watched him, her brow furrowing. Andy and Stewart always kept her up-to-date on what was happening with their family, and she'd attended more than one family dinner. She knew what Daniel's look was about... he could feel his beast inside of him, but it remained hidden in such depths that he was uncertain what it was, and he had not yet been able to shift.

They thought maybe it was because he lived in the vampire kingdom, and was surrounded by vampires all the time. Frieda couldn't help but think that maybe he was less shifter than vampire… and that the vampire side of him was going to win out in the end. She couldn't help but flinch at the thought. Especially after Stewart had just said that he'd rather be dead than be a vampire.

She shook her head and approached, trying to push those thoughts from her mind as she joined the others to hear what Typhoon had to say.

The alpha spread his arms open wide, the smirk on his face growing to an all-out grin. "Welcome, Cyclone, to the Savage Brotherhood."

Cyclone? Frieda's nostrils flared. Why was it that Stewart got a nickname right away and yet everybody refused to call her by hers? Her lip pulled back over her teeth, a snarl of disconnected disgust rolling through her. Well, maybe she should start telling everybody to call her Frieda—maybe then they'd actually call her Polaris like she wanted!

Her tail cricked in annoyance as nobody even paid attention to her irritation.

"You'll be placed on Frieda's crew," Typhoon continued, and Frieda's exasperation only deepened. "But understand that this is only a trial basis. You have to prove yourself a valuable asset before you are officially accepted into the Savage Brotherhood. Only then will you be given a rank, a designation, and a tattoo. Do you understand?"

Stewart barked and danced on the spot. Both Roxy and Twister shifted back to their human forms, laughing.

Typhoon rolled his eyes and let out a deep growl, which froze Stewart in place. Even so, Typhoon was grinning when he spoke.

"When I ask a question, I don't like to be barked at in return," he said.

Stewart's tail wagged in low, embarrassed sweeps until he shifted back to his human form. His muscular body was coated in sweat from the exertion. He bowed his head slightly toward Typhoon. "Thank you for this opportunity. I will do everything I can to prove myself a valuable member of the Brotherhood, and to get that designation as soon as I can. Before you know it, I'm going to be alpha of my own chapter."

The bold statement made both Frieda and Twister snicker, but in truth, it was something that Frieda could see happening. Stewart had involved himself in the Brotherhood for years now, not letting his humanity stand in the way of helping out every way he could. People liked him already, and he had a powerful presence. The only thing that held him back before was the fact that he couldn't shift.

That wasn't a problem anymore.

Typhoon rolled his eyes. "I decide who becomes alphas," he said, the growl in his voice deepening. "And I don't know if I like your attitude. One could easily take it to be challenging my authority."

"You know that's not what I meant," Stewart started anxiously.

Frieda started to laugh. She clapped her hands and shook her head, then pranced over to stand beside

Stewart. She elbowed him in the ribs as she grinned up at Typhoon. “Don’t you worry about a thing. I’ll whip this pup into shape before you know it.”

“See that you do.”

Typhoon turned to Mia, clearly finished. Frieda jabbed Stewart in the ribs again and jerked her head toward the tree line. “Want to go running?”

He turned to her, and she didn’t miss the way his gaze skimmed up her body, nor the way he hardened visibly. Perhaps that was the reason he didn’t answer—just shifted right back into his wolf’s form and took off, yipping over his shoulder as he headed for the forest.

Frieda grinned and followed him.

## Chapter Three

*Cyclone*

Everything glowed brighter in his wolf's form.

Boundless energy flowed through him, as though he had just woken up and drank a liter of energy drinks. Only it wasn't the awful, jittery kind of energy that came from too much caffeine. This was smooth, natural, the kind of energy he imagined he'd get if he was a plant in full sunlight. He bounced through the trees, his tail wagging in a circle. That was an odd sensation. Wagging his tail. It was as natural as grinning, but with muscles he never even had before. It almost felt like his butt was vibrating.

A full moon shone overhead, dappling the forest in shades of grey. Frieda kept pace beside him, her grey-brown fur almost silver in the night. She glanced at him, her tongue lolling from her mouth, and gave him a wink as she put on a burst of speed.

As much as Stewart was feeling the energy, his muscles were starting to ache a little, full of exertion that he had hitherto not been able to give. It was different running on all fours than it was on two legs, different to feel his paws sink into the earth than it was for his feet to slap the ground. Different… and wholly exciting. He yipped for joy as he tore after her, ignoring the burn in his muscles.

Eventually, though, he couldn't keep up anymore. He let himself flag back, then dropped to his belly and rolled on the ground, enjoying the mix of scents he found there. Frieda disappeared from view, but within a few minutes, she had reappeared. Her tail still moving in slow circles, she padded over to him and plopped down. Her sides heaved, and her tongue lolled. When she met his gaze, she winked again.

Stewart tried to wink back, but finding the facial muscles unfamiliar, all he managed was a blink.

Frieda rolled to her back, letting out a bark that sounded like a laugh. Stewart watched her for a moment. Just as in her human form, she was sleek and well-built. Muscles bunched under her fur, and her eyes glowed in the darkness. Her wolf form was smaller than many of the other wolves that Stewart had seen but no less powerful. She was strong, and what she lacked in sheer size, she more than made up for in speed.

He bounced back to his feet and tore off again, hoping to outlast her this time. Frieda soon settled into a comfortable trot beside him, and, recognizing defeat, Stewart slowed until he was at a speed he could keep up. They continued through the forest as Stewart enjoyed everything. The sight of the trees, the wind on his face, the smells he couldn't even identify.

However, there was one scent that was a constant beside him, one that he slowly became aware of, that one sweet scent that kept his nose twitching. He stopped dead and turned to Frieda, pushing his face into the fur at her shoulder to breathe in deeply. His suspicions were confirmed when her scent flooded his nostrils.

Frieda nipped at his flank, lightly, teasingly. A pressure started to build through his body and his lip curled back as he remembered the sight of her naked body. She was naked right now… though the sight of her wolf form did nothing for him, neither did her fur. He could still clearly visualize what she looked like in human form.

Sleek, with a compact, muscular body. Breasts that were just the right size, a hint of curve from her ribs to hips. An ass so tight you could bounce a quarter off it. He hadn't looked to see if she waxed or not, though… and now he found himself burning with curiosity. He turned toward her, his lips pulling back as he started to nip at her shoulders and neck; he'd seen Josef and Roxy do this a few times when they came back from running and had always thought it strange. Now, though, it felt completely natural.

Frieda leaned into his teeth, the push of her body against his forcing him to back up a step. She turned and jumped at him, her front legs turning to arms as they wrapped around his neck.

He hardened as she fell back, pulling him with her. As if on instinct, he shifted back to his human form. A thin sheen of sweat covered his body, making him shiver in the cool night air. Frieda's body pressed up against his, though, was warm and soft. His hardness pressed against her thigh as he pressed his mouth to hers. Her hands dug into his hair, her fingers curling into the tangles at the base of his neck. He thrust his tongue into her mouth, loving the taste he found there.

With a growl, he let his hands run all over her body. Her skin was smooth, marred here and there by a thin scar.

Her breasts were so soft against his hands, her stomach hard. When he slid his hand between their bodies to seek out her clit, he grinned against her lips and pulled back.

"I thought you waxed," he hummed in delight.

Frieda's eyes fluttered as he stroked her clit, but before he could do more, she grabbed his wrist, stopping him, and shook her head.

Stewart paused. His blood sung with need and he twitched against her thigh, wanting to be deep inside of her. He stared at her with an arched brow, asking without words. She had seemed to be into this minutes ago... what had changed?

"This is your first shift," she said slowly. Was she aware of the way her breasts pressed against his chest? "That means you've got euphoria going on. You're not in your right mind."

"No," Stewart protested, "I'm in my right mind. Finally. I've been holding back from you for too long. But I'm a wolf now, too. I'm not a weak human."

Frieda's eyes widened for a moment, but she still shook her head firmly. "No, Stewie. Not like this. When it happens, I want to make sure we're both in our right minds. Got it?"

Stewart let out a groan as he dropped his head to her shoulder. No, he didn't get it. He wanted her. He could feel by how slick she already was that she wanted him, too. But there was one thing he knew about Frieda—once she made up her mind, there was no changing it. So, if she had decided that they shouldn't do this right now... well... there was nothing he could do to change her mind.

With a reluctant grunt, he pulled back. Frieda gave him a sympathetic smile before she shifted back into a wolf and bounded off at once. Shifting took a little more effort this time than it had previously—his muscles already aching—but he was soon running after her.

It was only when they emerged from the forest to find his family still hanging out at the house that the rest of what Frieda had said hit him.

*When*. Not *if*. She had said *when*. He tilted his head to look at her from the corner of his eye. She trotted onward, heedless of him and the hope she had given him. A wolfish grin crossed his face and his tail started to wag again. *When.*

***

Daniel's first birthday was celebrated less than a week after Stewart successfully became a shifter. There was a lot of pomp and circumstance within Guinevere's kingdom, and Stewart was happy to see that Andy, Daniel and Guinevere weren't too tired that night to have a private family dinner at Josef's city mansion.

Once dinner was over, Roxy and Josef put their kids to bed while Guinevere and Andy cleaned up. Stewart slapped Daniel's back with a solid thump and gestured outside. They walked out onto the porch and Daniel slumped into one of the chairs set up there. He'd been quiet all evening, and out here Stewart could see the exhaustion lining his face, and the bruises under his eyes.

"Want to talk about anything?"

Daniel shrugged. "I had a checkup yesterday. Medically... I'm all grown up now. A full-on adult at only a year old."

Stewart's expression darkened and his grip on his nephew's shoulder tightened. Of course, that was something that bothered them all. Stewart tried not to worry about it—after all, what would worrying accomplish in the end? But it was always there. Daniel had grown from a baby to an adult in the space of a year. What did that mean for the rest of his life?

"Are the growing pains over, at least?"

Daniel nodded. “Yeah. I guess because I stopped growing, thank God.”

They stood in silence for a bit, staring over Josef’s walled grounds. Daniel had always been older than he looked, even when he was a little boy—for the few months that he was a little boy. Even as an infant, once Stewart thought about it.

“I’m sorry that you weren’t able to have a real childhood,” Stewart said slowly. “And I’m sorry that I wasn’t able to be the cool uncle and buy you things your parents said you weren’t allowed to have. Guess I’ll just have to satisfy myself with being the cool uncle with Roxy’s kids.”

“Uncle Stewie, you don’t have to be sorry. It’s not like anything you did could have changed it. It’s just biology.”

Daniel stood and stretched. "This whole day has been overwhelming for me. So much to do, so much for people to say to me. But if it's any consolation, over the past couple of days I have been thinking a lot about my life. And I can say for certain that you are, in fact, the cool uncle."

Stewart let out a laugh. "Oh, really? And why's that?"

"Because you were the one who encouraged me to be reckless from time to time. To pull pranks, even when I didn't see the point of them. To jump on my bed after I was told not to. To put underwear on my head and go running through the hallways yelling that the giant aliens were coming to get me. You gave me the opportunity to be an actual kid. At least, you gave me the opportunity to behave like one. So, you're the cool uncle."

Stewart patted his back, then let out a sigh. He knew that there was only so much he could have done, but those few things that Daniel had mentioned? It wasn't enough. Even if he hadn't grown up crazy fast, he was the son of a vampire queen. That alone meant he had to have a lot of decorum. Not to mention there were a lot of people gunning for him... to use against Guinevere, to use against the Brotherhood, or just because they didn't think that he should exist at all.

That was a lot to have to grow up with.

"Have you thought about what you're going to do?" Stewart pressed, turning to meet his nephew's eye. "I know for a while there you were talking about joining the Brotherhood. Is that at all on your list still?”

“I haven’t shifted yet. Dad and I are working on techniques to try to coax my wolf forward. But I can’t join if I can’t shift.”

Stewart grunted. “Don’t I know it.”

“I am certain the problem is that I live with vampires,” Daniel continued. His brow furrowed. “Or maybe it’s an unconscious battle between the two halves of me. I mean, I get fangs and a craving for blood easily enough. Maybe it’s just not going to be part of me.”

“Hey, kid, you’ve only been trying for a year. I’ve been fighting to become a shifter for a great deal longer. I’d be seriously pissed if you could just snap your fingers and get rid of your problems when it took me so long to overcome mine." He playfully shoved Daniel's shoulder, and Daniel relaxed with a smile and a laugh.

"Alright, alright. I get it. I can't give up just because it hasn't happened yet. But speaking of shifting. Now that you can, how are you going to prove yourself a worthy member of the Brotherhood? I wouldn't want to be around if you piss off Typhoon."

Stewart smiled cockily. "Typhoon isn't as terrible as he likes to pretend. After all, Dr. Mia's with him and she'd never be with someone who was a real toad."

Daniel rolled his eyes. "The kids have gone to bed. You can say bastard around me, you know. I'm not a fucking infant."

There was a part of him that was shocked to hear his one-year-old nephew saying such words. It was probably for the best, though. Daniel might not say it, but Stewart knew that he was a little stifled, living with his parents. They wanted to protect him from everything and that included being an adult and all the problems that came with it. Him pushing boundaries was the only healthy thing to do…

"Fine. She'd never be with a fucking bastard," Stewart said, grinning at his nephew. "And as for how I'll prove myself worthy to be a member of the Brotherhood? It's quite simple, you know. First, I'm going to follow orders and work to the best of my capabilities. Behave as part of the team and—"

A snort behind them made both of them turn. Andy slipped onto the porch, an amused light in his eyes as he seized Stewart around the neck and gave him a rough noogie. “Yeah, right. I’d like to see you follow orders, buster!”

“Hey!” Stewart punched his brother in the ribs. “Get off!”

To his surprise, Andy released him at once. His face got very pale as he stumbled back, gasping. Stewart flinched, reaching to help him sit while Daniel grabbed his arm, expression pinched.

“We’re going to have to get used to this new strength of yours,” Andy gasped out, whacking Stewart lightly.

Stewart scuffed his toes on the floor. “Yeah. Sorry, I didn’t mean—”

“It’s fine.” Andy inhaled deeply and waved a hand. “Now. Proving yourself a member of the Brotherhood. It's about a balance between following orders and taking initiative. Frieda's a good gal. As long as you follow her lead, you'll be good. She won't steer you wrong."

Stewart nodded. His mind drifted back to that night, when their bodies had been pressed together, the moonlight all around them and the smell of her arousal in the air. He understood why she had stopped them... it wasn't until the next day that he realized how affected by that first change he'd been. It was almost like being high, only there were no withdrawals coming down from it. He got why she decided to pull back, to stop them from going forward.

But Gods, he wished that she hadn't... It seemed like she was haunting him now, and the worst part was that she hadn't spoken to him. He couldn't help but wonder if maybe she had put a stop to it because she didn't want it... didn't want him... and now, somehow, he'd ruined their friendship with his lust.

"Yeah," he mumbled, glancing away. "I'll follow her lead. She knows what she's doing, after all."

# Chapter Four

*Polaris*

Stewart's eyes glowed as he took his place with the rest of the crew. A few of them whistled and several patted his back, murmuring congratulations. His ears turned pink, but a giant grin was spread over his face.

Frieda couldn't help but grin back at his excitement. It was clear that today was going to be something special. Part of her wished that it was a bit of an easier mission for their first time out with their new member, but there was no point in going easy on him. It might not be an easy mission, but it was straightforward and would be a good test of his skill. He'd be fine; they all would.

He grinned at her and winked. She turned away slightly, fighting the blush that rose in her cheeks—just that wink was enough to remind her of running through the woods with him. Their bodies pressing together. His hardness against her thigh. Oh, how much she wished she had been able to simply push aside doubts and enjoy the endorphins of a first shift with him.

But it remained fact that he hadn't been in his right mind, not fully. It would have been wrong for her to take advantage of it. Regardless if they had ended up having regrets or not, she would rather have no doubts for their first time.

If they ever had a first time. Frieda wasn't sure that it was going to happen. The moment had been so intense, and she longed for another moment just like that… but if there was one thing she knew, it was that sex changed things. You couldn't just boink friends and then go on as though nothing had happened. The nature of her relationship with Stewart had already changed. What if adding in a sexual dynamic changed it so much that they no longer worked well together?

Right now, she could run damage control. She could get them back to where they were before, and she wouldn't have to worry about things changing. The past year had seen a lot changing in her life already… Andy leaving the crew, the leadership of it falling on her, a half-vampire baby springing up out of nowhere. Heck, even Typhoon had gotten himself a mate and was shifting focus from the Brotherhood, slowly but surely.

It was all so much change already… could she really take more? Even if it promised to be as fun and exciting as Stewart? It was still change, and she still was uncertain how it was going to effect things.

Maybe the Brotherhood wasn't the best place for her, as hard a time as she had dealing with it. But that was different. The change of plans, the change of group dynamics, people coming and going, she could handle all that. It was the personal stuff, the emotional stuff, that she had difficulty with. She'd have been perfectly happy staying steady and stable for the rest of her life, thank you very much.

As she waited for the dawdlers to come in, she crossed the room and stood over Stewart. Friend or not, change or not, he was now a part of her crew, and she had to deal with him the same way she would deal with any other new member. She folded her arms and stared at him seriously. His cocky grin grew, and she felt heat starting to rise in her cheeks. Why was it that she could never be as stern as she wanted with him?

"Listen up, Cyclone," she said, keeping her voice flat. "This is your first mission, and it's an exciting time for you. Just remember that this is a trial basis. You're not a full-fledged member of the Savage Brotherhood yet. If I decide you're not up to scratch, that means you're out of here. Got it?"

Stewart's grin became somewhat serious, although not nearly as serious as it really ought to be. His smile stayed in place as he nodded. "I am well aware of that, Polaris."

Somehow, even though she wanted people to call her by her nickname, it always sounded teasing coming from him and she frowned.

"I intend to be the best newcomer that you've ever trained." Stewart winked at her and added slyly, "I'll do anything you want in order to get your approval for my graduation."

Why, oh why? Her core tightened and something inside of her fluttered at his tone. She wanted to return his grin and tease back, but now wasn't the time for that—for any of these unprofessional feelings. And so, her voice came out sharper than she intended when she replied. "I'm not going to be seduced into giving you a favorable report, Cyclone."

His grin faltered. “I wouldn’t dream of it.”

A small pang hit her, unhappy with the way he suddenly looked very serious. Apparently, it was a day when nothing was ever quite good enough for her. Still, she nodded stiffly and returned to the front of the room. The rest of the stragglers had arrived and taken their seats, and she flicked on the projector that would show the map of the joint they were going to rob.

“Alright, listen up,” she called to them, sweeping her gaze over the gathered group. She eyed each member of the crew, making sure they were paying attention. None looked so eager and bright-eyed as Stewart. He was practically humming with excitement, unable to make himself sit still.

*He knows what the gang does, and he has lots of experience in other matters. He has dealt with gang business before. The difference is now he's in on it from the start instead of being blindsided when things go wrong.*

"I want a clean mission," she continued, "Everybody stick to the plan and no improvisations. We go in through the sewers here and here. Lightning is in charge of the second group. He and his team will cause a distraction while me and my group drill through the floor of Thomas' Jewelry store. We get in, get out, and get away clean. Any sign of cops, we pack up and leave it for another day. Better no jewels than someone getting busted."

Nods answered her. Lightning, a buff lion shifter, leaned forward with a twinkle in his eye. He'd begged for this chance for months, and she had finally relented. He was good at causing distractions, after all. There was more than one mission where he'd caused a scene that was not intended. Best to put his talent to use.

Frieda glanced at Stewart again. He'd be with her on her team, where she could keep an eye on him. "Now we all know the rules. There are no vampires involved in this mission, so we do not shift. Got it?"

Nods answered her. Stewart looked a little put-out, as though offended that she felt the need to remind him for a second time—she had told him this when she first told him about the mission. However, it wasn't just him that needed the reminder. They'd been having trouble with 'sightings' lately, shifters who weren't careful enough and got themselves spied by humans. While not all of them could be attributed to Brotherhood members, Frieda knew that Typhoon was cracking down hard on them.

“Right. We all know what we have to do, so let’s move out.”

Frieda strode to the door as chatter burst out behind her. The excitement of a mission started to move through her blood, even though she fought it. Getting too excited would mean making stupid mistakes. They all went to their vehicles; the distraction team would be on their motorcycles, while the drilling team was using a white cargo van with tinted windows, with the name of a plumbing company plastered on the side.

Once they were off, Frieda started pulling on her disguise; coveralls, with a bright orange vest and a hard hat. Nobody would notice the work crew, not when Lightning and his boys were causing a ruckus.

"You didn't have to remind me that shifting's out of the question," Stewart whispered to her as they drove over a badly-paved road. I know the rules. Besides, I don't need to shift in order to get a good fight in."

Frieda rolled her eyes. "Don't you think I know that? Don't get cocky, Stewie. Cockiness gets people killed."

Like it had her brother. The idiot. She had heard the story of his death a dozen times, trying desperately to figure out some way that it wasn't his fault. But of course, it was his fault. No matter which way she looked at it, it always came back to that; it was his own bloody fault that he had gotten himself killed, and that hurt as bad as knowing that he was never coming back.

There was no way she was going to let that happen with Stewart. He was smarter than her brother ever was, she'd give him credit for that, but at the same time, he was new to his Wolf. It could be hard to control. The last thing she wanted was for the mission to go smoothly, only for him to end up shifting in front of civilian witnesses and end up getting himself torn apart by Typhoon.

There was little time to dwell on that, though. They soon arrived at the sewage opening twenty yards from Thomas' Jewelry. As they got out of the van and started setting up the pilon cones and Frieda grabbed the stop/slow sign in order to redirect traffic, her nerves started to jangle. Her gaze swept up and down the street. Sunlight glared off windows, and she was glad it was a sunny day—so people wouldn't think twice about the large sunglasses she wore to obscure her identity.

But there was something wrong. Her nostrils flared, and a familiar scent wrapped into her nose. Damn! She tapped Stewart's shoulder and jerked her chin toward the van.

"Everyone pack up," she ordered as she reached for the radio clipped to her belt.

Stewart's eyes widened. He started to pick up the cones, as the others did the same, working quickly. Confusion marred his brow, even though he didn't argue with her. Thank God. This wasn't the time for explaining, and she wasn't about to waste time setting him straight.

"Lightning, scratch the mission," she said through the radio, making sure to block her lips in case they were watching. "Cops are onto us."

"Cops," Stewart repeated, but at a fierce glare from Frieda, he snapped his jaw shut.

"Lightning," she hissed over the radio again. "Do you copy?" Her heart sank when there were two bursts of static. Their distress signal. "Fuck! Get back in the van, now!"

Even as they jumped in, the familiar face of Lieutenant Brad Duster came into view. His expression was twisted as he drove his plain car straight for them. Frieda snarled under her breath as she jumped back into the van and slammed the door shut. That ugly motherfucker had been dogging her steps for too long! And now he just happened to be at the sight of a job?

"Floor it," she yelled, and their driver punched the gas. They ripped down the road as sirens started to wail behind them.

They zipped down an alleyway, to where Lightning and the others would be waiting; or at least, where they should have been waiting. Instead, the sound of gunfire reached her. Frieda glared out a tinted window to find Lightning and the others pinned down in various doorways or behind their bikes, a wall of cops on the other end of the alley, firing rapidly at them.

"Time for some fun, boys." Frieda bit back another curse. Motherfucking Duster! She'd clean his clock good if any of her boys got hurt in this stunt of his! "Twist the van, block them off. Cyclone, Flood and Snowstorm, you guys shift and get your butts outta here. Don't argue! They're not going to be shooting at wolves and Typhoon needs to know what's going on. The rest of you, pick a partner with a bike and hop on. Get the hell out of here as soon as you—"

Before she could finish speaking, blood-curdling screams rose from the cops at the end of the alley. Her head whipped around to find half a dozen pale, gaunt men drop down among them and begin to rend the cops apart. Her heart stuttered in her chest.

"Vampires!"

Even as she shouted, Lieutenant Duster and a good lot of uniformed police pulled up behind them on the other side of the alley. Her heart sank down into her stomach, where the acid dissolved it within moments. Trapped. Her hands clenched. Cops and vampires on one side, cops on the other side. No matter what happened from here on out.... People were going to die, and the Brotherhood was going to get the blame for it.

“Change of plans,” she snarled and punched the driver’s seat. “Bust through them.”

The cops blocking off the opposite end of the alley were falling rapidly under the vampires. Duster and his men started firing, and Frieda didn’t waste any more time. As the van crashed through the vampires and cops fighting, she sprang from the back and threw herself onto the back of one of the vamps.

Trust them to make her fight alongside cops! She shifted at once, tearing through the bone and dry flesh of the vampire’s neck. It howled as she ripped apart its spinal cord; as it fell, she sprang at another. Howls and shouts rose from the other end of the alley; she spared a split-second glance to see more vampires dropping among Duster and his men.

She snarled as a vampire lunged at her, green venom collecting on its fangs. She dodged the bite, rolling over the ground to knock its feet from under it. It seized a cop and its fangs snapped together, towards the cop’s neck. Frieda rolled herself over again, clawing the vampire’s side as she did so. Something heavy fell over her; she snapped toward the vampire, but it was too late; its fangs sank deep into the cops' throat.

Frieda threw off the body that had fallen on her and caught the vampire's head in her jaws. She shook herself rapidly, snapping its neck before doing the same to the cop, whose eyes were wide as he tried in vain to stem the flow of blood; he was dead anyway, and with vampire venom in his system? It'd be a painful death.

A cry behind her once more made her turn. Stewart stood fighting a vampire. His clothing was torn, his face pinched with concentration as he traded blows. He hadn't shifted. Her heart suddenly made its presence known again by jumping into her throat.

The vampire punched Stewart in the gut, making him bend double. Frieda threw herself forward, hurtling toward the vampire as it lifted its arm to elbow him in the back of the neck. Her jaws clamped around the vampire's wrist, yanking it off balance. Even as she did so, though, a blade flashed in the vampire's other hand.

Pain erupted along her flank as the blade sank into her side. At the same time, bullets ricocheted off the walls around her. Chips of brick flew into her face. She twisted hard, flinging the vampire over her shoulder, then stumbled. Blood matted the fur on her side while Stewart punched the vampire in the face, and Lieutenant Duster screamed from behind them.

# Chapter Five

*Cyclone*

A hiss of pain brought Stewart's head whipping around to Frieda. She was on the ground, shifting from her wolf form back into human. Stewart grabbed the gun that he and the vampire had been fighting over and whipped around to shoot another two coming at them in the face; they went down as he dropped to one knee beside Frieda.

"Shift, you idiot!" she snarled at him. "There are vampires—"

"I got it covered." He glanced at the long cut in her side which was oozing blood. Not bad, so long as she stayed down and still. Not going to happen in this climate, he knew, but he didn't have time to think about that at the moment. He fired the gun at another couple of vampires, then chucked it into the face of another one. "We're getting blamed for this, aren't we?"

Pain flashed over Frieda's face. He didn't need to hear her answer. It was obvious. Probably why the vampires attacked at this point at all. Kill cops, leave evidence that the Savage Brotherhood was involved, and presto. They'd have even more cops gunning for them. Stewart wasn't going to let that happen, not if he could help it.

The vampires were starting to break away from fighting the Brotherhood, taking cops here and there with them. Frieda said something, but Stewart ignored her.

*So much for following orders.* He jumped to his feet, gave a vampire coming at him a roundhouse kick, then took off down the alley. Frieda shouted after him, and several other voices joined hers. None of the shifters were at this end; but also, at this end were cops who hadn't been killed yet. More than that, the vampires weren't paying attention to the fight happening at the other end of the alley.

Stewart sprang from the ground, calling his wolf forward as he did so. The shift was smooth, like slipping on a second skin. Fur sprang from his body; his teeth became sharp and pointed. Claws burst from his fingertips and his clothing shredded off his form. He hit hard into the back of a vampire, sending it stumbling forward.

A howl ripped from his throat as Stewart grabbed the arm of another vampire and yanked hard. He felt unwieldy in this form, unused to fighting in it; he shifted back to his human form, causing a vampire that had lunged at his flank to overshoot and run face-first into the wall. He allowed himself a second of amusement before he punched another vampire square in the face, then dropped to kick out the legs of another one.

He sprang back to his feet, already sending out a flurry of punches aimed at throats, kidneys and other weak points. The vampires seemed startled to find him fighting like this, and they were slow to counter his attack. It allowed him to get in close to one of the living cops, who was swinging a nightstick at his enemies with a determined scowl on his face.

Stewart grabbed the cop, spinning him from a long-clawed swipe at his throat, and shoved him toward safety.

The vampires hissed, one of them howled, and they surged forward. Stewart punched at the nearest one, but this was blocked. The vampire snatched his wrist and twisted sharply. Stewart let himself twist in the same direction to avoid getting his arm broken entirely. He bared his teeth with a snarl, using the vampire's momentum to throw himself into a second vampire.

He kneed a vampire between the legs, then shifted quickly back to his wolf form to snap his teeth around the throat of another. His muscles burned with exertion. They were starting to tremble, and he could feel himself slowing. Two vampires came at him from either side, and he just managed to slip through them—right into the arms of a third. This vampire wrapped its arms around his throat and began to squeeze.

Stewart sucked in a deep breath before the vampire's arm cut off all air entirely. He shifted and twisted, reaching for the vampire's face. From the corner of his eye, he saw Frieda grab the cop and usher him into a tight group of other shifters. Then she barreled towards them, her honey-gold fur bursting from her naked form as it shifted into that of a giant wolf.

His thumbs jammed into the vampire's eyes. They sunk in with an audible pop, and the vampire withdrew with a howl. Its arms loosened just enough for him to break free. Stewart weakly pushed the vampire away as he sagged against the brick wall, gasping for breath. Two more vampires came at him again.

Frieda barreled into them. She snarled. Stewart tried to push himself from the wall, but dark spots were starting to form before his eyes. He coughed, massaging his bruised neck. When he tried to push himself upright again, he found his knees couldn't hold him and he dropped.

Arms wrapped around his chest. He instinctively lashed out, but Lightning's voice hissed in his ear, "Easy, now!"

Stewart let himself get pulled away from the fight. Gunshots went off, people howled in pain. He felt oddly chilled, like he was in the dead of winter rather than a bright, warm day like this. Lightning hefted him onto his back and carried him back to the van and tossed him in. Moments later, Frieda was there as well, leaning over him, and they were moving.

"Cyclone!" She slapped his face. "Wake up!"

Stewart groaned. "I'm awake."

Relief washed over Freida's face. "Can you tell me where it hurts?"

"Right now? Where you slapped me."

"You're a real fucking riot, Stewie."

He rubbed his eyes and glanced at her again. She had put on a vest and a pair of shorts. A blanket was laid over his body, and when Stewart pushed himself to his elbow, he found that they had stopped moving. At first, he was confused, but then he realized what had happened. His cheeks turned bright red as he fell back with another groan.

"I passed out, didn't I?"

"Yeah, you did. Shifting a half dozen times in five minutes will do that to a body."

Stewart shook his head, ignoring the pounding he had just noticed, and pushed himself up again. Lightning sat near the back of the van, along with the cop that he'd managed to rescue. Stewart grinned at the sight of him, happy that at least *one* thing in this mess had turned out the way he wanted. That grin faded away entirely when he caught a full view of the utter fury on Frieda's face.

"Did we lose anybody?" he asked, sobered by her expression.

Frieda snorted and rolled her eyes. "That's the first question that you ask?"

"Well, yeah!" His brow furrowed. What was she so mad at him about? Was it because he'd disobeyed her orders during the fight? "Don't you think I'm concerned about whether or not anybody was killed?"

"He's got a point," Lightning pointed out, but dropped his head at the rage Frieda sent his way.

Frieda poked Stewart in the chest. "We haven't lost anybody. Yet. I'm this close to tearing your throat out myself, though. What were you thinking? Acting like a complete idiot! What, did you think you were being heroic by taking on all those vampires by yourself? And what for? To save a cop? Dust-Face Brad of all people?"

“Dust-Face?” the cop sneered at her. “I thought you’d be more imaginative than that, Frieda.”

“The name is Polaris!” She turned on him, the snarl and growl clear in her voice. Her teeth sharpened into fangs in her mouth and the cop flinched back. “You shut up before I decide to call up the vamps and hand you over to them. I’m sure they’d love your sugary blood.”

His already pale skin paled further, and he hunched his shoulders. From the way he held his arms, his hands were bound behind his back. Stewart studied him for a moment before turning back to Frieda. He had seen her in a temper before. True, it was never this intense of a temper, but that didn’t mean he didn’t know how to deal with it.

“Why are you mad at me?” Best to be direct.

“Why?” Frieda threw her arms into the air. “You risk your life for a fucking *cop* and you have the nerve to ask me *why I’m mad*? I told you to retreat! I gave you a direct order and you deliberately ignored me! You can forget about getting your tattoo, *Cyclone*, because after this I’ll make sure you never—”

“Chill out.”

Frieda’s face turned bright red, her eyes narrowed to slits and she seemed about to burst with fury.

“I didn’t risk my life just to save a single cop. I did it because the vamps were killing off all the cops, and they were doing it so that the Brotherhood would take the blame. They were going to have the cops breathing down our necks forcing us to fight a battle on two fronts. I saved Dust-Face there so that we'd have a witness for our side of things. So that we don't get labeled cop-killers."

Frieda's nostrils flared. She opened her mouth, then closed it again. Her shoulders slumped forward as the rage slowly drained from her face.

From the corner of his eye, Stewart saw Lightning's eyes widen. Even the cop seemed to be somewhat shocked as Frieda sat back and hid her face in her hands. Her dark tattoos stood out against her pale skin. Stewart clutched the blanket around his middle as he slowly reached out and traced his fingers over the dragon just above her elbow. She shivered at his touch, then lifted her head and glared at him. The venom had gone out of her look, though. Instead, she just looked tired.

"I get what you were thinking. It wasn't the best thinking, mind you, but you had the Brotherhood and the crew in mind." She shook her head and dragged her hands through her hair. "But it was an empty gesture, Cyclone. We can't use the lieutenant to sidestep the blame on this one."

Stewart frowned. "And why not?"

"Because," she snarled, her voice taking on an edge again, "he saw vampires. He saw us shifting. He knows too much."

Ice flooded Stewart's veins. He knew that they sometimes did hard things, but it wasn't like they'd kill a civilian for witnessing more than he should have... right? *Except he's a cop.*

*He doesn't count as a civilian. He might not be vampire or shifter but does that matter?*

"So... where does that leave us, then?"

"It leaves us holding a lieutenant prisoner. Typhoon's on his way, gonna try to figure this mess out. You know, we can say that we weren't responsible for that massacre all we want, nobody's going to believe us unless we let Duster here go."

"Which we can't do."

Frieda's face turned to a scowl as she nodded. "Now. Think you can walk?"

Stewart tested his muscles. "Yeah. I feel... pretty good, considering I passed out."

A ghost of a smile flickered over Freida's lips. "Good. Now help Lightning get the lieutenant to the holding cells, and I want you standing guard. You pulled him away from the vamps, he's your rcsponsibility until Typhoon gets here."

Stewart nodded. He fought the urge to salute—right now it was clear that he was skating on thin ice, and while normally that might make Frieda smile, he had a feeling that his humor would not be appreciated at the moment. He only hoped that when she calmed down more, Frieda would take back what she had said... surely his behavior hadn't been bad enough to be completely expelled from the Brotherhood... right?

***

He waited on guard duty for several hours before the lieutenant fell asleep. Like she was waiting for that moment, Frieda appeared shortly after. She gestured at him to join her across the hallway. Stewart sucked in a deep breath as he obeyed. There was tension in her jaw and shoulders still. Had Typhoon arrived yet? Were they going to kill the lieutenant for being a witness?

"Before you say anything," he started, "I have something to say."

Frieda folded her arms and studied him with a blank face before she nodded.

Good. Stewart took a moment to collect his thoughts, running a hand through his short hair. When he found a knot at the back of his neck, the sharp prickle reminded of when she had tangled her fingers there, and the taste of her lips on his. With a grunt of annoyance at himself for the swirl of desire that had him hardening, he slumped against the wall and folded his arms.

“We’re supposed to save lives. I know the Brotherhood isn’t all about protecting people against vampires. I know that we’re also big into the crime scene. Robberies, heists, drugs... even murder. I knew all that when I decided to sign up. But the thing is... our central purpose is supposed to be saving lives. Stopping vampires from preying on innocent people. Maybe if the world knew about shifters and vampires, we’d have a different sort of relationship with the law. Maybe not! But we have to be more than just crime, otherwise... Otherwise what good are we, really?”

Frieda didn't answer.

Stewart held his breath, waiting anxiously. Yet she still didn't speak. She was utterly still, her gaze slightly distant, her arms folded over her chest. Her expression was utterly blank. Usually, he was able to guess at least partly what was going on in her head, but not right now. She was completely unlike his best friend.

Was this what it meant to be part of the Savage Brotherhood? He was so worried about their friskiness in the woods coming between them. Should he instead have worried about his greatest dreams?

Eventually, her gaze flickered back to him. Still no expression.

"Come on, Frieda." His voice slipped into a tone of begging. Wow.

Where had that come from? He hardened his voice. “Just speak to me, dammit. If you’re still pissed, fine. Be pissed. But don’t just close off like this! You and I are supposed to be able to talk about things. If you’re going to start changing that now— “

“I’m thinking.”

Her tone was petulant, and Stewart let out a sigh of relief. “Well, think a little louder. I’m going crazy over here. I don’t want this to end up being the last hurrah of Frieda and Stewie. You’re too important to me for that... if you need me on a different team or—”

“Shut up.” Frieda smiled slightly as she shook her head. “You’re talking too loud for me to think. When you talk like that you sound like Twister.”

Stewart smiled proudly. There was nobody he'd rather sound like than his big brother.

Frieda sighed. "I don't want you on another team. And I'm not going to kick you off for that stunt of yours. I can't promise anything about Typhoon, but I can promise that I will fight for you. As for what you said... yeah. We are supposed to save lives. Sometimes, though, the lives that we save are ours. We always have to put ourselves first."

Stewart nodded, understanding what she meant.

"Now come on. Duster's secure enough in there. Typhoon's almost here. We can't leave him waiting."

Stewart cringed but nodded. No. It would not do to leave Typhoon waiting.

## Chapter Six

*Polaris*

It turned out that Typhoon didn't want to talk to them. Not at first, at least. So rather than them keeping him waiting, he kept them waiting. Frieda tapped her foot anxiously in the small lounge area of this particular safe house, alternating between deep breaths and not breathing at all. If Typhoon decided that this mistake was on her—which it was, as the leader—but if he decided it was a bad enough mistake, she could kiss good-bye to everything she'd been working for since she joined this outfit.

*I never wanted to be a leader. I was perfectly happy as second to Twister. Typhoon's the one who put me in this position.*

Soon enough, however, Typhoon came to see them. His expression was hard but not scowling like Frieda expected. Some of the tension left her shoulders, but she knew better than to allow herself to fall completely at ease. Typhoon glared between her and Stewart for a moment before he gestured for them to sit down. They did so, Frieda sitting on the edge of her chair in case she needed a jump up and protect Stewart… Or stop him from doing something stupid.

"This is a fine mess you've made."

Frieda folded her arms and didn't respond. He didn't sound angry, which was a good sign. She still didn't speak, though, waiting for Typhoon to pronounce his judgment. The alpha didn't look at her or Stewart, instead staring at the far wall with a pinch in his brow. Whether it was to judge their patience or gathering his thoughts, Frieda wasn't entirely certain.

Eventually, though, Typhoon blinked, shook his head and glanced at Stewart. "You're quite lucky. Lieutenant Duster seems to be quite understanding about the whole issue... apparently, he's seen a few things that have made him wonder about the illegitimacy of our organization for a while... Something about Frieda being too good to be a low-life criminal."

Frieda's cheeks went hot at the knowing glance that Typhoon sent her at that. What? Just because some cop thought she wasn't completely evil it meant something was going on? As though she'd ever go for somebody like Dust-Face Brad anyway!

"He has agreed to report a story back to his superiors which is favorable to us... And he won't be talking about vampires or shifters, either. Not that I blame him on that one. Who would ever believe him?"

Frieda let herself relax, finally. So that was that! There weren't going to be any complications with Duster, which was more than she'd expected. With that out of the way, it meant that Stewart's actions weren't going to be held against him. She started to smile, but when Typhoon's gaze hardened and snapped toward her, she tensed again.

*Fuck!*

"You, however... I thought you knew better than this. You are the leader of your crew and their safety should be your number one priority. So tell me why you ended up leading them straight into a trap? You should have known that the cops were onto you. Not only that, but vampires finding out where you'd be? That is sloppy work, Polaris. *Sloppy*. We have no room for that sort of incompetence in the Brotherhood."

Frieda flinched. Of course he'd refer to her by her nickname only when chastising her. She struggled to keep her face blank as she nodded. It was her mistake. If she had had the information that she should have had, then she would have known about the cops and vampires. She wouldn't have led her people into an obvious trap like that.

Stewart frowned. He opened his mouth, but Frieda jabbed him in the side with her elbow and shook her head, giving him a fierce glare. He glared right back but closed his mouth again. Frieda let out a slow breath, then turned back to Typhoon.

"I will get to the bottom of this right away. Find out how the cops and vampires knew where we'd be and what we'd be doing."

Typhoon hummed in his throat, then snorted and nodded. "You'd better."

He left quickly after that, taking Duster with him. Frieda let out a sigh of relief once she was sure he was well and truly gone. Slumping back in her chair, she passed a hand over her eyes. That was close. Typhoon hadn't been angry with them, but that didn't mean that he wasn't going to hold this against her record. Which was just as well... Maybe she'd be able to convince him to pull up a different leader for the crew.

Only, she didn't think she could be second to anybody but Twister, and he wasn't coming back. Not when his position had been expanded on and he shot up through the ranks.

It was several minutes that she and Stewart sat in silence before he spoke. "That guy needs to take a chill pill."

Frieda snorted on instinct. She couldn't recall anybody every talking about Typhoon that way before. When she glanced at Stewart, she saw that his face was twisted into a scowl. Part of her glowed at the concern he was showing toward her, but a bit of anxiety rose up in her at his words.

"He's right, though."

His head whipped around, and his mouth opened angrily.

"I should have been more careful. If the cops learned what we were planning on doing this time, they can find out what we're doing next time. Not to mention the danger that vampires pose. They're getting bolder, to attack us in broad daylight. They must be planning something big…" She trailed off, then shook her head. "But that is Typhoon's job to handle."

"He didn't have to attack you like he did."

"Attack?" Stewart nodded, but Frieda laughed. "That wasn't an attack, Stewart. That was barely a tongue-lashing. I've seen a lot worse when it comes to Typhoon. He doesn't hold back on letting you know when you've screwed up, but this? This was barely a slap on the wrist."

"He insinuated that he'd kick you out of the Brotherhood for it. It's not your fault, there has to be some sort of leak or—"

Frieda held up her hand. "If there is a leak, it's my job to find it before it leaks. Certainly before we end up in this bad a situation."

Stewart scowled. He didn't look convinced. Frieda looped her arm around his. She had been far harsher with him than Typhoon had been with her, and yet he was more upset about Typhoon. She felt herself smiling, even though she knew that it wasn't really the time. She couldn't help it. He was such a sweet guy.

"All Typhoon did was to remind me of what I already knew. No harm, no foul."

Stewart's scowl deepened. He folded his arms, difficult because Frieda didn’t release him, and leaned his head back. “I was the one who dashed into the middle of vampires. But he didn't even mention that.”

“He did.” Frieda arched a brow. “He told you you were lucky that Duster agreed to tell things our way.”

“So, when's the other shoe gonna drop? That's not going to be all that happens... is it?”

“I imagine it will be. Typhoon isn't the type to leave things unsaid.”

Frieda felt the tension slowly leave Stewart’s body. He relaxed against her and dropped his head to her shoulder. The move was so familiar that Frieda stroked her fingers through his hair before suddenly being reminded of that night in the forest... She inhaled sharply as heat swirled in her body. Maybe it was the relief of Typhoon's lack of anger... maybe it was the adrenaline finally fading... Maybe it was long-suppressed dcsircs merely refusing to be suppressed any longer. She swallowed hard. If she allowed things to go there, would she regret it?

She had been regretting *not* going there ever since the forest... she knew if she didn't make a move she would regret it... it just seemed like every time there was a possibility, she froze with fear of the maybes. Maybe it wouldn't live up to expectations. Maybe it would change their relationship too much. Maybe it would be better off being left unsaid and undone...

She was so wrapped up in the confused haze of desire and uncertainty that she missed his next words. “What?”

“I said, does that count for you, too? He's not going to charge back in here and tell you that he's decided you're out? He won't just take everything away from you?”

“No,” Frieda said firmly. “And if it helps, he's not going to do that to you, either. I know how much this means to you. And... while we're talking about it... I'm sorry for blowing up at you earlier. I shouldn't have called you an idiot. What you did, you did for the good of the Brotherhood. You risked your life on the chance that we were going to be able to get Duster to side with us. So, thank you. And I'm sorry for what I said.”

Stewart tilted his head, still on her shoulder but now in a position where she could see his smirk. "What's this? Polaris apologizing to one of her underlings? Careful, I might start thinking I'm special."

Frieda shoved him playfully. "Smart ass."

"Why, my ass is very smart, thank you." He winked at her, then brushed a tendril of hair from her face. "So, I guess that's the end of our first mission, huh? Other than me recklessly endangering my life and shifting far too much in a short period of time, how did I do?"

Frieda considered him for a moment. Normally when she had new recruits joining her team, she didn't let on to them how they did or where they stood in her ranking. And truth be told, she knew that the fact she knew so much about what Stewart wanted out of this had biased her, even if she worked hard not to let it.

Then again, she always made a point of getting to know the recruits and what their goals were. She patted his cheek and pulled away. “Not telling you that, Cyclone. Typhoon will get my report after the trial period is over. Nobody gets to know what I have to say before that. Got it, buster?”

“Buster?” Stewart frowned slightly. “Since when have I been a ‘buster’? Is this punishment for not listening to you?”

“Maybe,” she teased, batting her eyes at him. “But you know what? I like it. I think I’m going to start calling you buster more often, buster. It's got a great ring to it."

"Frieda—"

"I'm not telling you." She shook her head firmly. "Now. Since you've had your first mission, I want to get to know you a little better. I do this with all the new recruits, so don't feel self-conscious." Saying the words she said to all the recruits helped calm her. The heat still burned in her core, but she was able to ignore it. This was Stewart. She wasn't going to throw herself at him, especially not after the way she had made him cool his heels when he first shifted. "Tell me a little about yourself. Why did you join the Brotherhood?"

Stewart arched a brow at her. "You know why."

"Humor me."

Stewart let out a deep breath. He looked on the verge of refusing but eventually shrugged. “I’ve known about the Savage Brotherhood ever since I was a kid. I learned about them when a member of the Brotherhood came and saved me, Roxy and Andy from the vampire that killed our parents. Ever since then, I’ve wanted to be part of it. Andy might think it’s because I want to be like him, and that might be a part of it. Andy’s the best brother I could ask for and was more like a father to me in a lot of ways. But really, it’s more for Roxy. She gave up so much to keep Andy and I fed and housed. More than she lets on, I know. But I know she won’t let me repay her, not financially. And besides that, there really isn’t anything I *could* do to repay everything she’s given me. But as a member of the Brotherhood... I can fight vampires. I can try to stop other kids from going through what we went through. I can make the world a little safer, for her and for my nieces and nephews."

He'd told her this more or less ever since they met when he'd rant about being a human looking in from the outside. Not close enough to make real change, but not so far that he was out of danger, either. And as she had so often done during those times when she listened to him and ached to help, she slipped her hand into his. He squeezed it, his thumb gently coasting over the back of her hand.

Her skin tingled, and she found herself wanting to say or do something, anything, to distract herself from the pleasant images that started to circulate in her brain.

"Did I ever tell you why I joined the Brotherhood?"

Stewart nodded. "But you can tell me again."

Frieda shook her head, her gaze darkening as the memories came back. "My brother was a member. He'd joined for the glory, the excitement, and the money. He thought regular life was far too boring, and so he came hoping for something that would put his skills to the test. Well, he told me straight away that there were vampires. He didn't believe in keeping secrets from me, and he did everything he could to protect me. That meant making sure I knew what I was up against in life."

Stewart's thumb started to roll in circles a little higher, over her wrist.

“My reasons for joining aren’t as noble as yours. They’re not about protecting people or payback. Truthfully, I joined because it seemed like the only thing to do after he died.” Frieda shook her head and snorted. “He was an idiot, too. Got himself killed being an idiot. It wasn’t even against vampires. Maybe it’d hurt less if it had been. But in the end… it was a routine mission. He died… on a routine mission. Nobody should have died. They were robbing a bank, so there was danger there, but the security guard had willingly stepped down, so long as they promised not to hurt anybody.”

Stewart’s fingers tightened. “And he taunted the guard, until the guard snapped.”

“Yeah.” She shook her head and looked away. “It was his own damn fault.

After his death, I was so mad at him. But I missed him. So, I decided to join up. I thought in some strange way it'd keep him close to me. Or maybe I did it because I knew if he hadn't died, he never would have let me. Too dangerous. So, there you have it. I joined for uncertain reasons. But I've found my place among the Brotherhood. Fighting vampires has a certain feeling of accomplishment that comes with it."

"Not to mention you get to run with all these handsome motherfuckers," Stewart added unexpectedly. "I bet you have your pick."

Frieda's mouth went dry as she met his gaze and saw the desire in it. She swallowed hard. "Well… that's true enough."

"And here's one more. That you can take or leave." Hc moved quickly, as though to prevent himself from losing his nerve. He caught her face in his hands and kissed her, deep and passionate. Desire flared to life through her body. Her core lit on fire as she pulled him closer, closing her eyes as she enjoyed every sensation he sent spiraling through her body.

# Chapter Seven

*Cyclone*

Stewart would never know how they managed to make it back to his apartment. All he remembered from the time he kissed Frieda to when he slammed the door shut behind their bodies was the taste of her lips. The smell of her skin. The way her body pressed against him. The pressure inside his pants that was simply too much to resist.

Briefly, it crossed his mind that he probably ought to tidy a little bit, but that thought went flying when Frieda pushed him down on the couch and kicked the coffee table out of their way. Her hands flew over his leather, undoing each of the buttons before she pushed it off his shoulders. His own hands roamed her body. He wanted to feel every inch of her and was too impatient to wait for her to undress before he started.

"Oh, God!" Frieda let her head fall back when he started kissing her neck while pushing his hands under her shirt. "Fuck! Why did I take so long to start this?"

"You start?" Stewart chuckled into her skin as his tongue flicked over her pulse. "Are you kidding me? You want to take credit for my moves now? What are you, some sort of glory hog?"

Frieda tugged at the hem of his shirt, pulling it up to his armpits. Callouses snagged against his skin as she explored his torso, pulling away from his lips on her neck only long enough so she could bend down and begin to kiss and lick his chest.

"Good God," Stewart moaned, this time letting his head fall back. One of her hands pushed between his legs and massaged gently while the other started to work on his belt. "You've got a wicked tongue."

Frieda chuckled. Stewart let his eyes slide shut. He was actually throbbing under her touch, desperate to get free and find his way into her. One of his hands slid into her hair. He didn't want to talk, he didn't want to stay still. He wanted to turn her over and claim her every way that was possible. His impatience burned in his gut, but he forced himself to let her do as she wished.

When she stopped, he groaned with dismay.

“Before we go any further,” she said, looking up at him, “I need to know. You want this?”

“God, Frieda!” Stewart shook his head in frustration. “How can you even ask that? You’ve got the evidence that I want you right there in your hands!”

She giggled, but her expression soon grew sober. “You know what I mean, Stewart. This isn’t just a lust thing, right? It’s not two buddies deciding that fucking is a good pastime when they’re bored… right? It’s not going to replace us watching old movies together, or going to the beach or—”

“No.” His voice was gravelly as he met her gaze. “That will never change. You are more than a fuck buddy, Frieda. And I’m a little insulted you would think so little of me.”

"Well, when you put it that way… I guess I owe you an apology." Her hand moved again, slowly, over his clothed cock.

Stewart had a reply to that on the tip of his tongue, but it died away into a strangled moan as she undid his jeans and pulled them down to his knees. He was already hardened from her touch, and he stiffened even more when she bent over. Her lips grazed his head and her tongue flicked out, moving down his shaft. His one hand still clung to her hair, but he released her and fisted his hands at his sides. He didn't want to jerk and hurt her.

One of her hands moved up and down his inner thigh while the other continued to explore his torso, coasting over the contours of his muscles. He allowed his eyes to close, his hips jerking up rhythmically. When Frieda took him into her mouth, her tongue circling as she did so, both of her hands came to his hips and pressed him down firmly.

"Fuck!" Stewart gasped as she sucked, lightly at first but with increasing pressure. The pressure was almost too much to bear. He screwed his eyes tightly as she moved her head up and down, making greedy little slurping noises. His abdomen twitched with his building pleasure and soon he was breathing through clenched teeth.

Frieda showed no signs of letting up on him. She continued to suck his cock, easing him a little deeper every time her head went down. Part of Stewart never wanted this to end, to be inside of her mouth, to feel the gentle scrape of her teeth over his sensitive flesh. But another, larger part of him knew that he wasn't going to last much longer... and he wanted something far better with her.

"Fuck," he grunted again.

Frieda pulled back, her hands moving to stroke him inside of her mouth. She grinned up at him. "That's what I'm planning on doing."

She moved to take him into her mouth again, but this time he shook his head and stopped her. Even though the pressure was enough to make him explode, there was something he wanted—needed—first. He pulled Frieda to her feet, then stripped off the rest of his clothing. His eyes darkened as he started on her. First to go was the tank top. She wore no bra beneath, and so he immediately went to her breasts, sucking on one nipple then the other.

They hardened, pointing up towards the ceiling and his waiting mouth.

Next to go were her pants. The sweet scent of her arousal filled the air as he tossed them aside, then knelt so he could remove her underwear an inch at a time. It was her turn to clench her hands into fists. Her head fell back as he pushed a hand between her thighs. She clenched them on his fingers, but he still found her slick center. He grinned at her wetness, then glanced up at her and cocked a brow.

“Mind sitting down for me?”

Frieda let out a moan and collapsed to the couch. She spread her legs wide, lifting her knees over his shoulders. Stewart kissed her inner thigh, enjoying the way she shuddered. He slowly made his way up. She spread wider, opening up like a flower to him. His tongue flicked over her entrance. She was as sweet as he always imagined her tasting. The soft whimper that came from her throat was just as he imagined as well. A grin curled his lips as he slowly made his way to her clit.

It was already hard, and when he laved his tongue over it, Frieda's whole body gave a jerk. She lifted her hips, mashing herself into his face. It was so unexpected that Stewart pulled back with a grunt. He glanced up at her face and found it beet-red. She opened her mouth, but before she could apologize, he dove into her again. He kept his gaze on her face as he worked her clit. Her chest heaved, her eyes widened, and her jaw went slack.

"Fuuuuuck," she groaned, and Stewart grinned into her. He could feel his wolf in his chest, growling with pleasure. A sense of triumph and connection went through him. He'd imagined this for so long, he hadn't realized he feared what might occur if she didn't enjoy it.

But she was enjoying it. Her legs were starting to tremble, her knees jerking back and forth. Her back arched and she clawed at her own hair, panting and crying out in turns.

And that wasn't enough. With a slight snarl in the base of his throat, Stewart pulled back. He plunged two fingers inside of her, happy to find her soaking and ready. He moved her hips so she lay across the couch, then took up a position kneeling over her. Giving himself a couple strokes to get himself hardened again, he pressed against her entrance.

Frieda's hands moved up his arms. She sighed, and he looked up into her eyes as he pushed in. The pleasure he saw there echoed his own. Her back arched, her hips lifted, and her eyes fluttered shut. Stewart clenched his jaw against his arousal. She was so warm and welcoming. They fit together perfectly, like pieces of a puzzle.

"I'm not going to last long," he warned. "It's been a while since I…"

"Same." A shiver ran down her back, and he loved the pink flush in her chest as he started to move. "Oh, Stewart! I had no idea you were this big."

Stewart chuckled as he gently fucked her, then moved down so he could capture her mouth with his as he continued. "You've seen me naked beforc."

"Mmmm, but I never *looked.* On purpose at least."

He chuckled as he picked up speed. Freida's eyes flew open and she let out a strangled cry. The pressure inside of him was blinding now, pleasure coursing through him so powerfully that he could hardly keep himself in a steady rhythm. Her fingers scratched down his back and he kissed her again. Their mingled tastes drove him crazy. He could feel her clenching and releasing around him. With a wild roar, he jackhammered into her, the whole couch shaking with the force of his thrusts. She lifted her hips, matching him, her fingers now digging into his arms.

They flew apart on the same note, her clenching down on him as waves of darkness washed over his vision. He collapsed over her, his thrusts jerky and hard as she cried out, gasped and kissed him. Slowly they both became still and held one another. Stewart buried his face in her shoulder, breathing in the scent of sweat clinging to her skin. He finally registered the pain from her nails digging into him, but he couldn't bring himself to care.

Eventually, Freida let out the softest of sighs and stroked her hands down his back. "We can change positions so you don't have to hold your weight up like that. I can feel you trembling."

"Not because I'm too weak to hold my own weight."

"Never said you were weak."

Stewart pulled back anyway. They shifted their position on the couch, and he eased gently out of her. They lay face-to-face, she pressed against the worn backing and he on the edge. Her eyes sparkled and glowed as she stroked his face. Stewart's heart swelled, filling with so much warmth that he thought he might burst apart. How was it that after so many years, they had finally jumped across the breach? He knew without a doubt this was one thing he would never regret. He opened his mouth to say so—

The door opened.

Stewart twisted as Frieda gasped. He let out a bark of warning and saw Roxy, Andy, and Daniel for a brief moment before Roxy slammed the door shut. Peels of laughter burst from the other side. Stewart and Frieda stared at each other in horror.

"You'd better get dressed," Guinevere's lilting, languid tones came through the door.

"You should knock!" Stewart spat back. He rolled off the couch, casting an apologetic look at Frieda as he reached for his pants. She covered her face, shoving her fist in her mouth to muffle her giggles.

Stewart grabbed her clothes and threw them at her. Shifters might not think much about nudity, since it was something that was going to happen from time to time, but having his family walk in on him having sex? Ugh! *Well, at least we had finished the sex.*

Frieda continued to giggle madly as she threw on her clothes. Stewart dressed quickly and dragged his fingers through his hair as he strode for the door. By the time he reached it, his face was no longer flaming red, and instead, a scowl stretched across his lips. What were they doing, just walking into his house like that?

"I told you we should have called," he heard Guinevere say just before he yanked open the door.

"You should have," Stewart agreed. He held the door open for them to come in. Frieda had gotten her giggling under control by now and nodded to each one of them as they entered.

To his surprise, Andy looked furious. He poked a finger into Stewart's chest. "The hell do you think you're doing? Both of you! You shouldn't be doing that."

"Chill out, Twister." Frieda rolled her eyes. "As though you never fucked with any of the crew before."

"That's different—"

Stewart stepped in front of his brother. "We're both adults and we make our own choices. You don't get to say what we should and shouldn't be doing. What are you doing here, anyway? This is my place now, you don't get to just walk in without even knocking!"

"It's my fault, Uncle Stewart," Daniel said. His hands were shoved into his jeans and he shrugged, looking a little red around the ears. He looked up at the ceiling, as though too embarrassed to look at Stewart directly.

"You said I could come over any time, so I thought it'd be fine if we all just came over... Mom said we should have called."

Stewart let out a breath, trying to calm himself. If it was any other situation, he wouldn't have been angry at them for just walking in. Honestly, this was as much his fault for not locking the door. People in his family rarely knocked or told each other ahead of time when they were coming over. It just wasn't something they did. He dropped to the couch beside Frieda while the others found spots to sit. Andy still looked furious, but when Guinevere gave him a stern look, he shrugged and sat as well.

"So, what brings all of you here, anyway?"

Guinevere and Andy exchanged another look. The rest of the anger faded off of Andy's face and he sighed. "Daniel."

Stewart twisted to look at his nephew. Just as he opened his mouth, though, Roxy started talking. Daniel shut his mouth, annoyance flashing over his face.

"We're all dead certain that the reason Daniel has not been able to fully tap into his shifter side is because he's surrounded by vampires all the time. So, he's decided that he wants to live around shifters more. Since you're family and you've already got various security systems in place," she nodded at the door; this whole floor of the apartment building had various shifters associated with the Savage Brotherhood living on it, "we decided it was the best place for him. And we think it's going to be good for his personal growth, too, not to have to be the prince all the time. Being able to be a little more anonymous."

Stewart turned to Daniel. "Is that what you want?"

"Yeah. Well, I thought it might be better if I had my own place but—"

"But that is far too dangerous," Guinevere interrupted. She put a worrying hand on her son's shoulder. Pain flashed in her gaze even as she tried to hide it. "But he'll be safe here."

Stewart met Daniel's gaze. He saw the frustration there and nodded slightly to show that he understood. Daniel was a grown man, both physically and mentally. It was only natural that his parents would fret a little, but this? It was coddling him. He understood where they were coming from.

On the other hand, it was a good idea for Daniel to come live here. It'd let him have some independence. "Yeah, that'd be fine. I'll get a key made for you."

Daniel dipped his head toward him. "Thank you."

"Yes," Andy said, a little suspicion slipping back into his voice. "Thanks. But there is something else that we—"

"No, we don't have to talk about it," Frieda said flatly. "Stew, I gotta hit the road. See you later."

Stewart nodded at her. They shared a quick kiss, and then Frieda left. He sighed as he looked back to his family. This was going to take some explaining.

## Chapter Eight

*Polaris*

When Frieda got a call from Typhoon telling her to come to headquarters to speak with him, the first thought that ran through her mind was that Twister ratted her and Stewart out. Technically what they had done wasn't against the rules, but Typhoon frowned very strongly on relationships between people on the same crew. It was even worse because Frieda was Stewart's supervisor.

Typhoon would be furious with her. Probably put Stewart's training to a different crew.

She walked into headquarters with her head held high and her gaze steely. She wasn't going to let him intimidate her into being ashamed. What she and

Stewart had done was no more than what others did... She wasn't going to let her judgment be clouded just because of her feelings for him!

When she strode to stand before Typhoon's desk—it always surprised her just how office-like his office was; he truly ran the Savage Brotherhood like a military business—he didn't look up for several moments. She could see his nose twitching, though, and bit back the urge to tell him to just spit it out. He'd speak in his own time.

Eventually, he set down the pen he was using and looked up, folding his hands on the desk. "I have never known you to fuck one of the new recruits before."

For some reason, even though she had been thinking of what she and

Stewart had done as fucking, the way Typhoon said it made her hackles raise. Maybe it was because of his tone. He made it sound so animalistic. There was so much more than lust in what they'd done, though.

Typhoon sighed as he stood. "I have always said that mates make my people crazy. I had hoped you were above that, Polaris."

"Above it?" Frieda snorted. "You make it sound like there is something shameful about having a mate. What's Mia going to say?"

"Leave Mia out of this." He glared at her for a moment, but a slight smile tugged at his lips. "Your point is taken, though. I'm not happy with you sleeping with Stewart, but I can't say I'm surprised. However, that does make what I am about to say have a bit more… edge, I suppose you could say, to it."

Frieda sat when he gestured her to sit and nodded.

"I am going to give you and Cyclone a mission. It's going to be dangerous, there's no question about that, and if you're caught I will deny all knowledge of it."

Ice started to creep into her veins. "So, like a black ops thing?"

"Exactly. You and Stewart are going to assassinate King Rudolph."

Frieda blinked. Then stared. Then blinked again. Her thoughts tumbled over one another as she struggled to process what she had just been told. King Rudolph. He was a vampire king over near Oakvale. His kingdom wasn't especially large, but it was wealthy. What in Hell's Fires did he do that Typhoon would want him dead?

"So you want us to die?" The question came out spitting. "It's against the treaty! And how are we supposed to get close enough to a vampire king to kill him? Is this because I called you Bobby once when we first met?"

"I assure you, it is not."

Frieda threw her hands into the air. "Then why? What did I do? What did Stewie do? What could we have done that is so bad that you want us dead?"

Typhoon sighed.

"Not only that, but when Guinevere and Twister find out that you sent us to our deaths, they're not going to be happy with you, either. So, you're going to antagonize the only vampire allies that the Brotherhood has and—"

"Calm the fuck down." Typhoon glared at her. "You've got a good head on your shoulders. Stop acting like a hysterical woman."

Frieda's nostrils flared. Her eyes narrowed, but she sealed her jaw shut. Hysterical woman? He tells her to go on a suicide mission and then calls her hysterical when she is upset about that? And not just any suicide mission, but a suicide mission with someone who wasn't even a full-fledged member of the Brotherhood yet! Stewart could handle himself in a regular fight, but to go into the vampire's nest?

"You calm now?" He arched a brow at her.

That question alone was almost enough to make her lunge at him swinging, but she held herself back, keeping her ass firmly seated in her chair. “My question still stands. This is suicide. And no matter how much you can deny having any sort of knowledge of our involvement, the fact is it’s going to come back to bite the Brotherhood on the ass. What’s going on here? It’s not like you to throw the baby out with the bathwater.”

“Nobody is throwing anything. You and Cyclone have the best chances at this. You are quick on your feet and fast in your head. And quite frankly, Cyclone being Guinevere’s brother-in-law gives him and you the best chance at being held hostage should you fail, rather than being killed outright.”

She wanted to be furious about that. Wanted to tell him that was a relationship that they couldn't touch. She kept her mouth shut, though. Blowing up at Typhoon, especially since he was already writing off her feelings on the matter, wasn't going to help anybody.

"Rudolph is planning something big," he continued. "I can't share all the details with you, but the attack on your crew was set up by him. He wants to bring vampires out of the shadows, and now that he knows how to make them human enough to resist sunlight, he's been experimenting. My sources say he might be close to finding a way for vampires to keep all their abilities with none of the weaknesses. He's like most of the vampire kings in that he thinks they ought to be ruling over all of us."

Frieda felt a chill steal down her spine. There were plenty of vamps that thought that way. She thought it must have something to do with the fact that they had to kill humans to survive. It twisted something in their brains; how could they survive the guilt if they saw humans as equals?

“So, you want Stewart and I to kill him before he gets there. But if he’s having it researched, then shouldn’t we be going after his scientists?”

“He is his scientists. He’s had tons of schooling and always keeps his notes in his head. He’s paranoid about it being stolen and the glory taken by someone else. So you kill him, you end this threat.”

Frieda tapped her fingers against the arm of her chair. Her eyes darkened.

Over the past few years, things had been going up and down with the vampires. It seemed like every time they got a leg up on the leeches, they rallied back in another sector, throwing everything out of sync again.

“We need to just solve this once and for all!” Frieda snarled. Her hands bunched to fists. “We can’t keep running around like headless chickens, plugging up one hole only for two more to spring open. It can’t keep going on like this.”

“We agree on that one.” Typhoon pinched the bridge of his nose. “And I am working on it. For right now, I need you on damage control. If humans were to find out about vampires and shifters, it would be utter chaos.”

That was for fucking sure. Frieda slumped in her chair. Most shifters themselves didn't know about vampires. Those who did find out generally had some pretty intense reactions, and that was with one foot in the world of the paranormal already. With humans? It was even worse. Sure, one human here, another human there, they could deal with that. But the whole kit and kaboodle? Not a chance.

Which brought her to another thought. "Brad Duster. Can we trust that he won't say anything?"

"We'll have to." Typhoon's voice grew hard again and he dropped his hand. "Because the last thing we need right now is an increased cop presence in our way. Now. I don't want to know how you plan to kill Rudolph. I want you to go back to Cyclone and the two of you can figure it out on your own. Don't mess up. I won't be able to help you if you do."

***

It took three days for Frieda and Stewart, having intense conversations in hotel rooms and parked at make-out spots to avoid drawing suspicion, to put together their plan. Frieda wished that they could have more time than that, but from what she heard from Typhoon, even the three days was pushing it. On the third day, they told Daniel that they were going to have a weekend camping trip. He waved them off, shaking his head and telling them that his dad found the whole situation weird but that he was happy for them.

They drove all day and night to get to Oaksvale, then camped overnight in the forest. Neither slept well and so relaxed themselves by making love until dawn when they finally both fell asleep for a few hours. When they woke, they left their camping gear where it was and hiked up the mountain.

When they reached the barrier separating vampire territory form Brotherhood land, Frieda paused and turned to Stewart. “This is going to be unpleasant. You need to keep your wits about you.”

“Don’t worry. I’ve got a handle on it.” He smiled at her, that cocky smile that she found so reassuring she couldn’t even tell him not to get cocky.

They knew where to find the entrance to the underground kingdom, a slit in the side of the mountain that would have been unremarkable except for the utter darkness within. As there was no good way to lure Rudolph from his kingdom, the only way to get at him was to crawl into the beast's belly. Frieda's stomach wound itself into a series of knots as she reached for his hand. She was pretty certain the vampires already knew they were here.

But from here on out? This was what was going to be the true test. The plan was lunacy, she already knew that. Chances were they weren't going to survive this. She only hoped that Rudolph would be curious enough as to why a couple of shifters would walk into his kingdom that he didn't have them killed right away.

*The things I do for the Brotherhood,* she thought grimly. "Are you ready?"

Stewart nodded, his expression grim.

She bumped his shoulder with hers and, hoping to lighten the dark look on his brow, whispered. "I wish we had time for another stretch before we go in there."

The tension lightened from Stewart's brow. He turned toward her with a grin and reached for her hand. "Oh, really? If I had known that, I would have put you up against every tree we saw since we crossed that blasted barrier."

The image of her against the rough bark came to her mind. She could just imagine herself, half-sitting in some branched-off area, Stewart kneeling before her while her glistening parts were open for the whole world to see.

There was something appealing about that imagc, really… A giggle started to build up in her throat, and she quickly stuffed her fist into her mouth to stifle it. Her eyes flashed a warning to Stewart, but he only smiled and leaned in closer.

“First,” he whispered, tracing his hand over her hip, “I’d spend a little time just kissing you. I’d stick my tongue in your mouth and only when you started rocking your hips and grinding against me would I move my hands from your sides. I’d feel my way up your body, testing the weight of each soft breast before pinning you in place and ripping off all your clothing. I’d catch your gasp in my mouth. Then I’d find your pulse.” Here he put his hand around her neck, two fingers pressing into her pulse, which was going pretty fast already. “And I’d find your clit. I’d stroke it into a little hard nub, and then when you were panting and moaning, I'd—"

"What makes you think I'd let you get there without my own actions?" Frieda interrupted. Her whole body seemed to be on fire and her voice was breathless. If it wasn't for the possibility that a vampire was watching them right now from the inky darkness, she would have suggested that they find a tree right now. "Before we got to that point, I'd be ripping off your clothing myself."

Stewart hummed, then shook his head. "No, not for this fantasy. Don't get me wrong, I like you taking control. I really like it," he winked, "but there are times when I'm going to be the dominant one. Only as far as you are comfortable, of course, but I do want to dabble with some BDSM once this is over."

And if it ended with them dead? Frieda pushed that thought away. They'd just have to survive it. That's all there was to it. "I have never tried BDSM. Can't say that I haven't thought about it from time to time, though... Never found anybody I trusted enough to try it out with, I suppose..."

One of his big, warm, strong hands cupped her face. He bent in close and brushed his lips across her cheekbone. "It's a date then."

Frieda nodded, breathless once more. "Yeah. Once this is over, we'll get some cuffs and ropes and whips..."

"Sounds good."

They stood there staring at each other for a long time. Frieda could see in his eyes there was more he wanted to say. She wanted to say more, too. She wanted to tell him things she had never told anybody before. That he was her best friend, that she would give up everything if it meant she could be with him forever. That her feelings had run deep and true for a long time. That if he was still human, she wouldn't have been able to hold herself back anymore anyway.

"I..." Could she tell him that she loved him? Would she have regrets if she didn't?

"I know. I do, too."

Warmth spread through her body. She threw her arms around his neck, pulling herself so close to him that their clothing hardly seemed a barrier at all. Their mouths crashed together with a hungry ferocity. Teeth clinked together as Stewart's hands roamed all over her body. She didn't even care if there was a vampire in the darkness watching now. They'd been here long enough for a whole gaggle of them to be waiting. She didn't care. She just wanted this last kiss. Full of the passion and words that she couldn't speak aloud.

When they finally broke apart, the two of them stared into each other's eyes, clinging to one another for a long moment before they stepped back. Then, holding each other's hands, they descended into darkness.

The sunlight quickly faded as they entered the long tunnels. The smell of blood and rotten fruit surrounded them, and Frieda breathed through her mouth so as not to smell it. Her heart pounded wildly in her chest as her eyes struggled uselessly to adjust to the utter black. There was no sound around them, not that it made a difference. In this darkness, vampires could see as well as day and with their flying abilities, they didn't have to make a noise.

She squeezed Stewart's hand tighter as they continued. And she couldn't help but wonder what they had gotten themselves into.

## Chapter Nine

*Cyclone*

The pitch darkness around him made his hair stand on end. Stewart fought against his wolf, growling and snarling in his chest. It wanted to come forward, to take control of his body and tear apart the unseen threats in the black. He was well aware of Frieda beside him, her warmth, her scent, the soft sounds of her breath. He clung to her hand in a way that a pulse throbbed in his fingers, but whether it was hers or his or both he wasn't sure.

"So…" He whispered, unable to stand the silence anymore. The vampires probably already knew they were there, after all. "Do you think we'll come to some light soon?"

“Honestly,” Frieda sighed, sounding a touch put-out but he could tell it was due more to nerves than anything else, “We should have brought a flashlight. It’s not like we could evade the vampires for very long, anyway.”

A chuckle sounded from right behind them, making the hair on the back of Stewart’s neck prickle. He whirled, even though the tunnel behind them was as pitch-black as the darkness in front of them. A cool breeze brushed over his face and he could just imagine a vampire leaning forward, lips pursed as it breathed outward at him. He snarled and swiped at the space before him, but his hand hit nothing.

“A bit late for that, don’t you think?” the voice came from above them now. “What are two shifters doing strolling so casually into a vampire kingdom? Not just strolling casually, but knowing that they are entering a vampire kingdom… One would think that you have a death wish."

Stewart snarled again, tugging Frieda a little closer to him. She gasped, and he whirled, pulling her tightly into his arms as he growled at the unseen threat. Frieda elbowed him in the chest, growling herself.

"Cool it," she snapped at him.

The vampire chuckled, this time right before them. "This is interesting. So she's the one that does the mounting, eh mutt?"

Stewart worked hard to get himself back under control. He could not flub this up. *Keep calm and don't panic.* It was cliché, but it was what he had to remember to do right now. “We want to see—”

“I’m sure you do.” The vampire interrupted and laughed. “Luckily for you, my king wants some new shifters for his latest experiments… and you have to be living for his purposes. Hold out your hands and surrender and I’ll take you where you can see. Otherwise, I’ll have to kill one of you to make the other behave. Is that going to be necessary?”

Stewart snarled again. His wolf told him to shift, to find the fucking vampire who dared threaten Frieda and tear him apart. However, this was their plan… being taken prisoner by the vampires so that they could get close to the king. It had seemed like lunacy before, but now it was downright stupid. Why had he agreed to this again?

“I don’t suppose we have a choice,” Frieda said dryly.

She gently removed her hand from his and he could sense her holding her hands out. Reluctantly, he did the same. His eyes hurt from squinting in the darkness so hard. His hands clenched as bands of cold metal snapped around his wrists. Once more he had to wonder at how wise this course of action was, but it was too late now. The metal was right against his skin, and he knew that he wouldn’t be able to break free if he tried.

One hand rested on his shoulder, warmer than he expected, and propelled him into the darkness. Frieda’s breathing stayed even beside him, so he knew she was still there, but it didn’t mean that he was any happier with the situation. He kept his footsteps timed with hers, breathing in her scent and reminding himself that she was alright.

Light stabbed into his eyes so suddenly that they began streaming and stinging instantly. Stewart flinched back, squinting as the white light burned against his retinas. By the time his eyes adjusted, the vampire had dragged him forward and thrown him into a chair. It was only then that he realized it wasn't just one vampire... There was a good dozen of the creatures around them. All chalky-white, with gaunt features and waxy skin.

He glanced at Frieda at once, making sure she was still there. She looked a little nervous, but her expression was hard and determined. He released a soft breath and faced the vampire standing before them again. He was slightly shorter than the others, stockier. Surprisingly, his face was covered in scars. A chill stole down Stewart's spine. How much fighting must he have done in order to *scar*?

The vampire looped his thumbs into his belt and considered the two of them. A small smile spread over his face and he shook his head, chuckling. "This was not what I was expecting today. It's times like this that I love my job… Tell me, shifters, what are you doing here?"

Stewart glared at him a moment before he remembered that they weren't supposed to be antagonistic. It was just difficult, with that guy's smug face and the feeling of danger prickling up and down his spine. He glanced at Frieda. She didn't speak, and so Stewart did.

"We came here to deliver information. It will be very *valuable* to the king." He emphasized the word valuable, so that the vampire would know exactly what they were after—or at least, pretending to be after.

The vampire arched a brow and leaned forward, his gaze sweeping from Stewart to Frieda, then back to Stewart. "Valuable information, you say? I hope it's not just your sexual preferences. As interesting as it was to hear about how you want to tie up this lovely puppy here and fuck her senseless, the king is centuries old… hearing about your kinks will be nothing new."

Stewart's lip curled back from his teeth. So, the vampires were listening. And calling Frieda a *puppy*? Infantilization much?

"What sort of information do you have?" the vampire continued, this time focusing on Frieda. "I know you. You're a member of the Savage Brotherhood. So. Do you have information on Typhoon or has he sent you here on one of his little schemes?"

Frieda tossed her head back, her long hair flowing down her back. It had been done up when they entered the tunnels. Stewart's wolf howled and raged as he realized that the vampires must have let it loose. What else had they done? He hated the thought of them touching her while he was mere feet away, oblivious to it all. A snarl started to work its way up his throat, but she shot him a look. He forced himself to quiet.

"We have valuable information," Frieda repeated. "And yes, it does have to do with the Brotherhood... and your king's experiments. But we won't negotiate with anybody but him."

The vampire's brow arched. "Negotiate? You think that you can negotiate with vampires, sweetie? Oh, my… Aren't we full of ourselves?"

Stewart frowned. "If you want our information then we will only speak to the king."

"Speak to the king," the vampire repeated in a mocking voice. "Well, now I know Typhoon isn't the one that sent you. He'd never be so stupid as to send a couple of his people to my kingdom without even letting them know who I am."

Stewart's eyes widened. His head jerked toward Frieda instinctively. She looked just as shocked as he felt. This was King Rudolph? Hadn't Typhoon told

Frieda, at least, what he looked like? Stewart had assumed that she would know the king on sight… apparently, they hadn't discussed everything in as much detail as they should have. He could have kicked himself.

This mission was suicide. He already knew that, but now he was beginning to feel it. Maybe, if he shifted, he'd be able to hold off the vampires long enough for Frieda to get out. She had a good nose; she'd be able to track the path they took back out of here.

But before he could even start to try to shift, Frieda spoke. Her voice was cool and calm. "Well, your Majesty, it is an honor that you would choose to interrogate us yourself. Now, as for the information that we have—"

Rudolph's hand snapped out. It slapped over Frieda's face with a smack, causing her head to jerk back. She cried out and Stewart lunged. Several pairs of hands seized him and thrust him back into his chair. White fur started to creep out from his skin, and he barely choked back a growl. His eyes narrowed to slits, though.

"A woman's mouth is good for only one thing," the king sighed, sounding bored. "And it's not talking. Don't you agree?"

Stewart snarled, hating the way this bastard was talking about Frieda. At the flash in the king's eyes, though, he forced himself to relax. The vampire guards still held him in place, but their grips weren't quite as tight. He forced himself not to think about ways he could break free and pulverize the king as he stood thcrc...

"I said, don't you agree with me?" Rudolph narrowed his eyes at Stewart.

He sucked in a deep breath. "Well, I suppose that depends. Polaris here does have a problem knowing when to shut up sometimes."

He could feel her glare boring holes into the side of his face but didn't dare look at her. He knew he was going to have hell to pay for that comment, even if he was just playing along with Rudolph for now. Hopefully, she would understand... The king at least seemed to be appeased. A smirk came over his face as he leaned back on his heels. He, too, flashed a glance at Frieda, and Stewart wondered if this was more about humiliating her than anything else.

A growl started to work into his throat again, but luckily, he was able to stop it from becoming full-fledged.

"Now. What is it that you two have brought to me?" Rudolph focused on Stewart again. "In all the years since the Savage Brotherhood formed, I have only known a dozen shifters willing to betray their own kind. Since Typhoon took over, it's become even less. He's a clever boy, that one, and I've never been able to figure out where exactly he's come from. So. How did it happen that you two decided to turn on him and he didn't kill you before you had a chance to get here?"

Stewart inhaled deeply. He couldn't be certain that Rudolph was telling the truth about this. In any case, they had worked out their cover story, as well as the information that they were going to feed the vampires.

"You know Polaris. So you know about the attack that vampires made on her, where they wiped out a bunch of cops. Well, Typhoon decided to throw her under the bus. He was going to hand her over to the cops, as though she was responsible for those deaths. If that happened..." He bunched his muscles and growled under his breath. "I'm not going to sit back and watch her take the fall when it wasn't her fault. If Typhoon won't protect his own people, then I have no use for him. He's always talking about doing what has to be done, taking care of business. But when there is something that he can actually do to help? He acts as though it's not his problem."

Rudolph cocked his head and studied him.

Stewart met his eye. “So… if he’s going to hand her over so easily, then he can go fuck himself. We need money, so that we can disappear from this place. Go to Argentina or somewhere. Get away from Typhoon and his tyranny so that we can live our lives together in peace.”

“That is quite the story. Except I know that there was a cop who survived and is blaming a new gang in the area.” Rudolph smiled. “So. Try again.”

“I know that cop survived,” Stewart snarled. “But that’s not good enough for Typhoon… I know that he—"

“I’m not an idiot,” Rudolph interrupted. “You have something else up your sleeves… Or did the female tell you that Typhoon was going to hand her ovcr? This reeks of feminine wiles…" He leaned over Frieda and cupped her face in his hand. "Did you bring him to me for some reason? Not as a bodyguard, otherwise you wouldn't be ticd in my chair… Hell, you wouldn't have even come in the first place. You'd have sent him by himself. So what are you up to?"

"I've already told you—" Stewart started.

Rudolph held up a hand. He glared down at Frieda for another moment before he turned on his heel and grinned at Stewart. "I don't think she's going to say another word when you're here. I'll have to find out how willing she really is to deal with vampires in another way, I suppose."

Images of Frieda tied down in a bed while Rudolph stood over her flashed through his mind. Stewart didn't even care if that wasn't what the king was thinking of. He reacted on instinct, his form half-shifting as he lunged at the king. Rudolph didn't even blink. Not that he needed to. Even as Stewart moved forward, the guards reacted.

A fist rammed into his stomach, causing him to choke and collapse to his knees. The chair clattered away as the guards took turns hitting and kicking him. Rudolph chuckled as Stewart curled into himself. He tried to protect his stomach and face. The metal cuffs bit into his wrists. Pain washed through him as the blows rained down.

"You need him." Frieda's voice was utterly unconcerned when it broke through the pounding noise.

The blows continued, making Stewart grunt and groan with each one.

"You *need him.*" There was no worry in her voice, only firmness.

Rudolph sighed. "Stop."

The blows eased off. Stewart couldn't help but groan in relief, even as the pounding in his head continued. His wolf snarled at him to shift and attack the vampires, but he held back. The cuffs were digging into his half-shifted wrists, and he could only imagine the damage they would do if he tried to shift all the way. He swallowed and peeked through swelling eyes to see Rudolph and Frieda staring down at each other.

"And what do I need him for?" the vampire asked, sounding bored.

"You'll see."

Rudolph snorted. “And how do I know that you’re not saying that to protect your mate? You shifters… you’re always so soft on the ones you *love*. It’s almost tragic, if it wasn’t so disgusting.”

Frieda smiled. It was a chilling smile that Stewart had never seen on her face before. “He’s not my mate.”

It almost made him flinch. He opened his mouth, a protest catching in his throat. He stopped himself just in time, though. One of the guards nudged him and a shot of pain went up his spine. He grit his teeth and held in everything he wanted to say. Frieda was just playing the game—and honestly, didn’t he deserve it after what he’d said about her before?

“Get him out of here,” Frieda continued and then smiled. “And then we can find out just what uses my mouth has."

His stomach plummeted. A snarl ripped from his throat, but before he could do or say anything, the king had gestured, and he was dragged to his feet by the guards. They yanked him from the room. The last thing he saw of Frieda and Rudolph was the king pulling her to her feet, a wicked smile on his face.

# Chapter Ten

*Polaris*

Frieda struggled to keep her expression blank as Stewart was dragged from the room, groaning low in his throat. Her wolf snarled at her ribs, wanting her to jump up and defend her mate. Wanting her to prove to the world that the words she had just spoken weren't true. It had hurt more than she thought it would, saying that he wasn't her mate. She hadn't even considered the possibility that Stewart was her mate... there was some part of her, deep in her heart, that had known for what seemed like forever. She had just never consciously thought about it before.

But of course, he was. Saying that he wasn't went against every fiber of her being.

Rudolph wasn't about to listen to them, though, so she needed to fall back onto plan B. This was going to be more difficult than she had originally thought. In her life, she had had to do a lot of things for the Brotherhood. Things that she didn't like to think about but had been necessary in the end. She only hoped that she could actually make this believable.

The king pulled her to her feet by the cuffs around her wrists and stared into her eyes, his own baby blues glittering. "Well, then. What uses does your mouth have?"

Frieda kept her face blank, hiding the way her skin crawled at the look in his eyes. Most vampires thought it disgusting to even consider any sort of physical interaction with shifters that didn't involve killing them. It was clear just looking at Rudolph that he didn't have the same sort of qualms. Well, she would deal with that if it came to it. At the moment, she needed to make sure that he believed her when she spoke.

"Many uses. One of which is speaking," Frieda said pointedly.

She tugged her hands free from him. There were still a handful of guards in the room; she wouldn't be able to attack and kill the king. Not yet. She needed to get him at ease first. Her stomach clenched as she thought about offering her body up for that, but the way he was acting, he'd probably just have the guards watch.

No. It wasn't going to come to that. She would not let it come to that. Yeah, she had done a lot of things for the

Brotherhood, but letting a vampire inside hcr? Fuck that noise.

"I didn't come here just for money," she said, keeping her gaze locked on the king's. She forced herself to keep her face blank. This was going to be difficult... but the alternative was even worse. "And I didn't come here to go against the Brotherhood. Not just against the Brotherhood, at least." She lifted her chin. "Typhoon's a beast, and I have no loyalty to him. Sure, this latest attack worked out in the end that I wasn't punished for it, but that doesn't mean he hasn't reacted in other situations. But I am here because of Guinevere."

The king's brow rose. He seemed to be taken aback, and Frieda allowed herself to smile at that. Her heart pounded against her ribs, her hands going cold even as she fought to keep herself steady. After a moment, Rudolph nodded at her and gestured at one of the guards. He came forward and unlocked the cuffs before retreating. Frieda rubbed her wrists, sighing in relief. She could shift and kill him now, but that wouldn't do her much good in the end. No, she had to keep patient.

"What about Guinevere?" Rudolph asked, sitting on the edge of his desk.

"Her... *mate*," she spat out the word as though it was poison. "Doesn't belong to her. Twister was my superior for years. He and I were mates. And it wasn't just sex," she added, hands clenching, trying to bring forward all the hatred that she didn't feel—but needed to show in order to pull this off. "He loved me. I loved him. And then she bewitched him and stole him away from mc. Just because…"

She turned her face away, feigning hesitancy to continue.

"Because what?"

She pitched her voice low, into a reluctant whisper. "Because she had his child… and I'm infertile."

Silence. Frieda didn't dare look at the king. Her stomach churned. If he didn't believe this, then they didn't have much left. He said he needed them for his experiments… the thought made her feel even sicker to her stomach, but it would at least ensure their survival, right?

"I see," Rudolph said. His voice was oddly gentle. His fingers brushed her cheek, making her look at him again.

"Well, I can see why that would make a female like you angry enough to come here... but what could you possibly offer me that would hurt her? I know about that half-shifter abomination. The only reason it should be allowed to exist is to learn how to make vampires stronger."

"It shouldn't be allowed to exist at all," she snarled back, recalling what a few members of the Brotherhood had said before she straightened them out—with force. "She ought to be burned at the stake, and he... If her bewitching wouldn't end at that, then it would be a kinder fate to kill him with her."

The king smiled and laughed. "Ah, yes. The true fury of a woman scorned."

She ignored the sexist remark. She had heard plenty worse in her time. She had a feeling that he wanted a reaction from hcr more than anything else.

"That doesn't tell me what you can offer me to use against Guinevere and her shifter mate."

Frieda looked back at the king. Her wolf snarled, warning her not to speak, but what choice did she have? She ground her teeth together for a moment, then glared at the king, wishing she could just tear out his throat at this moment. It wasn't just her own life that she was concerned about. If she killed him now, it was a sure thing that Stewart would be killed as well.

"The man I brought to you, as you so cleverly deciphered, isn't just some random shifter. He's Twister's brother. Guinevere's brother-in-law. Twister loves his family dearly, and I am certain you can find a proper use for Stewart."

Rudolph's eyes widened. His jaw started to hang slack before it snapped back. He jerked his head toward the door and one of the guards slipped out. "If what you've said is true, then it will indeed be of use to me. And if you're lying, *you* will be of use to me."

Frieda rolled her eyes. "It's the truth. Now let's start talking about my reward. Argentina is off the table… I want to retire in the French Riviera. Everyone knows that you have money. All I want is a little splinter of that."

The king grinned at her. "Well. We can talk about that for certain. But first, let's move to a more comfortable location."

***

Frieda had to admit, the king's personal chambers were every bit as lavish as she expected. Everything, it seemed, was gilded in gold. Velvets, silks, satins, it was all there. Rich, deep purples highlighted with red and amber. It was almost enough to give her a headache, really, and she had to wonder if the clashing colors meant that Rudolph was color blind.

Not that she asked it out loud. Instead, she said a few complimentary things about the room before they sat down and started to negotiate. In the end, she was promised half a billion dollars. It was more money than she had ever heard of. The only person she knew who could possibly have half a billion to give away was Hurricane—and she wasn't entirely certain that he would be able to toss it aside so easily.

A guard slipped into the room and moved to the king's side sometime later. He whispered into Rudolph's ear in what sounded like German, and Rudolph's face broke into a wide smile.

"Well, Polaris, it turns out you were telling me the truth. My men have just informed me that the shifter you brought in is, in fact, Stewart Franks. Brother-in-law to Queen Guinevere. This is quite a boon for me. I don't act like it's enough to make her hand over her half-breed child, but there is plenty else I've wanted from Guinevere that she has always refused."

Frieda inclined her head. She didn't ask what it was that he wanted, nor did she *want* to know. "How soon can I get my money?"

Her heart started to pound a little harder again. She was running out of time. How was she meant to get the king alone long enough to kill him? And after that, how could she get Stewart out alive? She tried to force the panic down. After all, they had yet another backup plan. It hinged on whether Rudolph would inform Guinevere about his capture right away, though…

“Soon enough.” Rudolph waved his hand carelessly. “Right now, though, I think you and I should get to know each other a little better… I have to see how willing Guinevere is to give me what I want, after all.”

“So you’ll be ransoming Stewart soon, then?”

“A message was already sent.”

Frieda frowned—when had he had the time for that? She didn't ask, though. Her hands were starting to go cold again, and with a prickling at the back of her neck, she realized that all the other vampires had slipped out at some point. Her breath started to catch in her chest, even as she tried to force herself to breathe evenly.

"Our business deal is done. What reason could we have to get to know each other now?" She prayed that her voice wasn't trembling too much. She needed a little more time. If they were going to get out of here alive, there needed to be time for Guinevere and Twister to act... "You have Stewart. You'll be able to blackmail Guinevere into doing whatever you want with him. There is nothing more for—"

"Oh, but there is."

Frieda pressed herself into the chair she sat in as Rudolph poured two glasses of wine. Her wolf snarled at her to just end him. *Not yet.* But what if she lost her chance? Her mouth was dry, her mind switching between the horror of what would happen if she missed her opportunity to the horror of what he clearly expected.

"There's more that I'm not entirely certain of," the king continued. He lifted his gaze to hers, his eyes smoldering as he offered one glass to her. "Is it just revenge and money you're after? And how does Typhoon really figure into all of this? You were quite vague about why you hate him, after all..."

"I don't—"

"Take it." Rudolph growled, pressing the glass into her hand. "There is no reason this has to be unpleasant for you, Polaris. You're a lovely female and I like you. I want to know more about you."

With a cold hand, Frieda took the glass. She didn't even pretend to drink, instead narrowing her eyes at Rudolph. It couldn't be clearer what he wanted now. Did that mean she had more time to do what she came here to do? Or did it mean that he would be expecting her to attack? That he planned to use physical force on her? And was prepared to put her down if she did try anything?

"I only joined the Brotherhood to honor the memory of my dead brother," she said, and to her relief, she didn't sound half as scared as she felt. "That's not a good enough reason anymore. Especially not with Typhoon."

"And what did he do to earn your contempt? You let him fuck you, too?"

Frieda hissed between her teeth. Her hand clenched. "Sex isn't the only motivation women have, you know. I have had to work twice as hard and be twice as successful in my career as the men I've served under and he still acts as though every little mistake I make is proof that I shouldn't even be in the Brotherhood. Not to mention the way he lets the men harass all the women like me trying to carve out a place for ourselves."

Rudolph laughed. "And you say it's not to do with sex?"

She glowered back at him.

"If you're so concerned about the other females in the Brotherhood, why aren't you doing more to help then, rather than running to the French Riviera?" Rudolph sipped at his wine and leered at her. "I could help you put Typhoon in his place."

"Typhoon really isn't worth that much to me."

Rudolph smirked. He strode casually across the room and peered at his reflection in a mirror, picking at something invisible beside his fangs. Was that a veiled threat? Frieda set the glass aside and got to her feet. This wasn't happening. Even though she shivered, and her stomach cramped, she wasn't about to let herself start thinking that it might.

"Just give me my money and I'll be out of your hair."

"Oh, but you haven't even gotten into my hair yet." Rudolph turned and grinned at her. Were his fangs getting longer? He glanced at her wine, then lifted his own and drained it. "You've told me the truth, *Frieda*, and I keep my word when I give it. I promised you money. But when did I ever promise you'd leave my kingdom? I have been thinking… it would be beneficial to have a shifter around. Permanently, I mean. There's only so much I can do with the ones that I bring in and cut open."

Her chest started to heave as her stomach clenched tighter. Was there enough time for Guinevere to mobilize yet? She knew that there were massive tunnels connecting the various kingdoms below ground, but was there enough time for her to get here already? Vampires moved fast—but that fast?

"I don't think you'd enjoy having me around." Her throat was so dry that her voice came out cracked. “I can assure you that I’m not worth this trouble. You’re a king, I’m sure there are others that you would rather spend your time with, besides a shifter.”

“You being a shifter is part of the appeal. Now. Will you take your clothes off or shall I tear them off you? I’ll say it again.” He grinned at her. “This doesn’t have to be unpleasant for you.”

He came at her so fast that she barely had time to flinch back. The next thing she knew, he had her pressed against the wall, her wrists pinned to either side of her head. Everything froze in that second, the pressure of his fingers on her wrists so tight she knew they’d leave bruises. She stared at his gleeful eyes, her lungs unable to expand properly as she stared at him.

"You weren't expecting that, were you?" he crowed. "Expecting me to be like the regular vampires?"

"You've experimented on yourself," she realized, her voice hollow to her own ears.

"That's right. You shifters can give us so much. We were originally one species, you know. Evolution separated us, the way it separated us from humans. But your specific gifts can propel vampires to our next stage of evolution."

He was faster than other vampires. Stronger. She didn't need to ask exactly what he'd done to know that. No vampire should be able to hold a shifter down like this. Her blood pumped in her ears and she lunged forward, bringing her wolf forward. Her teeth scraped against Rudolph's throat—and then she was slammed face-down on to the floor.

Fangs pierced the back of her neck. She felt the venom enter her bloodstream. Her wolf howled and thrashed, but it was already taking effect.

"You'll be begging for me soon enough," Rudolph hissed into her ear. "I hope you'll be more reasonable next time."

He released her, and Frieda reached to press her hand to her gushing wound. The venom spread through her body, fiery and burning. She screamed in pain—and the next sound she knew was glass shattering.

# Chapter Eleven

*Cyclone*

Stewart grunted as the vampires dragged him to his feet again. He wasn't certain how long he'd been in the dark dungeon cell, or if he'd fallen asleep or not. What he did know was that he felt a lot better now than he had when he'd been put in. It still amazed him how quickly he healed now that he was a shifter. However, he didn't want to let on how much better he was feeling, and so let out an exaggerated moan. One of the vampires lifted him off his feet and carried him a few steps, back into the light.

"What's going on?" he grunted, letting his feet drag as the vampire pulled him along.

"The king wants you to see," the vampire who was half-carrying him replied, not looking at him. "Gods, I hate it when he does this."

Does what? A chill stole down Stewart's spine. He opened his mouth to ask, but one of the other guards gave him a light punch to the kidneys; not enough to really hurt but enough to remind him to stay quiet. His heart started to pound. What had Rudolph done to Frieda? What were these guards doing, where were they taking him?

*Frieda is fast and strong,* he told himself. *She can defend herself against a vampire.*

But against a dozen? If Rudolph wanted something, would he care about an audience? Or would he maybe even find it more exciting to have people watch? The thought made Stewart sick to his stomach. His wolf snarled, and he acted on instinct. His whole body seemed to ripple and in the next second, he felt himself changing shape. Fangs and claws and fur. He lunged for the vampire that had hit him, ripping himself from the hold of the other one.

His teeth snapped on air as the vampire backpedaled. The one who had been helping him let out a shout and jumped on top of Stewart's back, wrapping one muscled arm around his neck and squeezing. Stewart's breath choked out. He twisted in the vampire's grasp and the arm only tightened further. He clawed at the arm.

And then the thought came to his mind, if he tore open his wounds again here, or if he was injured too badly now, then how was he supposed to fight later?

He knew that Guinevere was meant to mobilize her army and come after them as soon as she received word that they'd been captured… But things could always go wrong, and he needed to be at full strength, just in case…

He let himself go limp. The guard held on a little longer, then hissed in his ear. "Shift back. I know it's against your nature, but you can't save her if you're dead."

"What are you muttering about?" one of the others demanded.

The guard punched him in the kidney, sending pain flaring through his body. Stewart grunted, but slowly shifted back to his human form. His mind whirled. Was this guard going to help him? He said he hated it when the king did this... could it be possible that this was the final straw for him?

The vampire dragged him back to his feet. "You gonna cause more trouble or you gonna be reasonable?"

Stewart forced himself to go a little limp. He leaned against the vampire heavily. Another of the guards pulled a set of cuffs out, but his guard waved them off.

"If he tries anything we'll just beat the tar out of him."

The other vampires laughed at that. Stewart tried to suppress a growl, though he wasn't entirely successful. It didn't really matter. It earned him a half-hearted slap, and then they continued on. His nerves were on edge, every scent and sound seeming to ram itself into his brain. He wanted to throw off the vampire and go tearing off to find Frieda, but he still had that uncomfortable sinking feeling in his chest that they were taking him to her already. And he wasn't going to like what he found.

The guards dragged him into a dark room. At first, he was confused until he saw the window showing into a separate room. Frieda sat on a couch, and Rudolph was nearby, pouring out wine. Stewart's mouth opened slightly, confused, until he realized what it was... a two-way mirror. So, Rudolph intended to make him watch...

He snarled and got a fist packed to his ribs for it. The scene unfolded, and Stewart found it increasingly difficult to stay still—and when Rudolph bit her, he couldn't. With a howl of rage, he threw himself at the window. The guard released him, crying out as though in pain. Several of the others dodged in, grabbing Stewart.

Frieda cried out, pressing a hand to her wound as she fell from view. The vampire king laughed, looping his thumbs into his belt as he stared down at her. He said something, but Stewart didn't hear what it was.

He punched a vampire in the face, then whipped around to sink his fangs into the arm of another one. He twisted sharply, throwing the vampire over his shoulder and into the mirror. It shattered, and Rudolph turned, eyes widening. Stewart leapt through the broken glass, ignoring the shouts behind him. All he cared about was getting at Rudolph—and then getting Frieda out of here.

Rudolph grinned and easily sidestepped his attack. He grabbed Stewart by the neck and flung him over his shoulder. Stewart hit the ground hard. The king struck out rapidly, so fast that Stewart couldn't see his hands move; it was just blow after blow centering on his chest and stomach. His heart stuttered under the force of the blows.

Stewart rolled, shifting back to human form. As he hoped, Rudolph wasn't expecting that; Stewart was able to grab the base of a broken wine glass and jam it up into Rudolph's jugular. The king jerked back instinctively; Stewart shifted again and latched his jaws around the king's head. With a mighty wrench and tear, his teeth cut through flesh. The guards all leapt on him, fists pounding against his body, but it was too late. With another wrench, he took off the king's head.

There was a long, frenzied howl from behind him. The guard who had helped him before abandoned the fight, dashing for the broken mirror. A few of the others looked around, and then Frieda was on them. She tore apart two before Stewart even understood what was happening. Her eyes were almost fully black, a terrible snarl on her lips as she pounced on another vampire. Stewart's heart gave a lurch; she was going rapid, the vampire venom turning her mind to the basest of instincts.

He flipped over, keeping out of Frieda's way as she picked off stragglers. The rest of the vampires tried to hold against her, but it was clear they were in a losing battle. Stewart retreated and watched as Frieda tore through them like tissue paper. The sickly sweet smell of rotten fruit increased until it burned in his nostrils. Frieda tore apart the last one with a savage snarl, then whirled around. Her black eyes focused on him and she lunged.

Stewart flipped to his back, showing his belly. She skidded to a stop, a look of surprise coming over her expression. He twitched, she snarled, and he took a deep breath. As human, she'd tear him apart in seconds.

But if he didn't get her calmed down, she was going to die. The venom would kill her. He exhaled slowly, then let himself shift back to his human form. He stayed laying on his back as he reached out to her. She snarled a warning.

"It's okay," he whispered.

Memories flashed through his mind. His father reaching out to his mother just like this, her black eyes roving in her head. Madness and pain making her muscles twitch and her body jerk. Right before she killed him, and then herself. Sometimes he wished that his father had just left her, grabbed him, Roxy and Andy and fled. Now he knew why that had never been an option.

"It's me, Frieda," he continued to whisper, moving a little closer. "I know you're scared. I know you're in pain. It's the venom. It's making you go rabid. If you let me, I can suck out the venom. Let me help you, please. Please, darling. I love you. I can't lose you."

Frieda gave a little shiver. She backed away from him, shaking her head. A whine came from her throat. He knew she could turn against him in a second but didn't let that stop him. He slowly moved to his hands and knees and crawled toward her.

"Please," he breathed. "Let me help you."

Frieda trembled. She dropped to her belly, whined, and shook her head. Stewart quickly moved to her side. The wound in her neck was crusted with green venom, but he ignored the disgust rolling around in his stomach and bent over her. The venom was the worst possible taste he could ever imagine; there was no comparison. It made him gag, his stomach churned, and he retched several times.

But he kept sucking until he could taste her blood, clean without the taint of venom. She still shook, and he knew that the effects of the venom would not so easily fade, but it was as good as they were going to get.

Frieda moaned as she shifted back to her human form. Her naked body was covered in sweat and she shivered madly as Stewart gathered her into his arms. One of her hands pressed briefly to his cheek, then it dropped again. Her eyes rolled into the back of her head. Stewart's chest burned with the need to get her out of here.

He stumbled to his feet, an exhaustion in his limbs that hadn't been there when he'd jumped through the window. Because he was shifting so often, or because he'd ingested some of the venom as he sucked it from Frieda's system? It hardly mattered... he pushed past the ache in his legs and headed for the door. It was locked, and he had to shift Frieda in his arms in order to turn the deadbolt. Once the door was open, klaxon alarms started to blare.

Stewart flinched, stumbled, and picked a direction. He started running, not caring if it was going to take him to the entrance or not. He just needed to get out of here!

A dozen guards rounded the corner ahead of him. One of them gave a shout and started after them as he wheeled about. The vampires flew into the air, streamlining themselves as they came after him. Stewart threw himself to the floor. Frieda moaned as he tucked her into a corner, praying none of the vampires went after her while he was still fighting.

He bounded to his feet, aiming a punch at the nearest vampire's face. He missed; to his surprise, the vampire didn't attack him. The whole lot of them flew past. Stewart's head whipped around to see two dozen vampires wearing Guinevere's crest crash into Rudolph's guard. He sagged against the wall, blinking several times.

A hiss sounded in his ear, and he turned to find one of the guards hovering over him. Stewart groaned, then threw himself forward. He wasn't giving up, not when help was finally at hand!

"Stewie," Frieda moaned as his fist connected with the vampire's face. "Stewie...."

His heart stopped as she went utterly limp. No! Not now! He turned on the vampire and redoubled his efforts, his fists flashing through the air. He wasn't going to let go… not now… not ever…

*Hang in there, Frieda. Please!*

***

It took them three hours to get out of Rudolph's kingdom. After Guinevere's army showed up, he had carried Frieda with him as they made their way out. By the time they were finally free, he had been on the verge of collapsing. Once they made it back to Guinevere's kingdom, he had collapsed. He woke only at the sound of Frieda's moans and found Dr. Mia bending over her.

At first Stewart's instinct was to snap at her to leave Frieda alone, but luckily, good sense prevailed. He sat up, watching anxiously. Mia glanced at him, gave him a half smile, and returned to her work.

"She's going to be fine. I've administered an anti-venom. Her vitals are all good." Mia covered Frieda with a blanket. "My mate is here, if you want to talk with him."

Typhoon? At first, Stewart didn't think he'd want to talk with Typhoon at all... but as the events that had happened, and what had almost happened, crashed down on him, he found himself snarling like a beast. He sprang to his feet and stalked out of the room—lavish, but tasteful, like all of Guinevere's décor—into a separate apartment space. Typhoon waited there, hands laced together.

"You had no right to send us in there," Stewart roared, barely stopping himself from lunging at Typhoon. "Do you have any idea what almost happened?"

"Almost," Typhoon returned calmly. "I am sorry for whatever you went through, but if you're saying something *almost* happened, then I have to assume that it *didn't* happen."

Stewart balled his hands into fists. "It was an impossible mission and you—"

"For an impossible mission, you certainly did well."

"Don't start playing games, Typhoon." Stewart snarled as he came at Typhoon, about ready to tear his fucking head off. Typhoon hardly even blinked. The sheer power and force of being alpha made him intimidating. Stewart's wolf wanted to submit, even though Typhoon hadn't done anything overtly threatening yet. He pushed that urge aside, too furious and too afraid of what might have happened if he hadn't gotten to Frieda in time. "He was going to rape her. You should have warned us that—"

"What?" Typhoon's eyes widened. He got to his feet. "Are you serious?"

Stewart fell silent. He was too blown away by Typhoon's seeming not to have known the threat levels to make a response.

Typhoon glanced over Stewart's shoulder at the door. He let out a shaky breath and shook his head. "Vampires generally pride themselves on sexual purity. Humans are okay in a pinch, but they see sexual acts with shifters as little more than bestiality. I had no idea... Fuck!" He ran a hand through his hair. "I didn't even consider... if I had, I would have sent you with someone else."

Stewart frowned. "Me?"

"You were the only one with some measure of immunity. Everybody knows about Guinevere and Twister. As his brother, you're prime for being kept alive as a hostage. Nobody else has that." Typhoon stared at him hard for a moment, then sighed. "You've earned a place on the Brotherhood, if you want it. You might even be alpha material. Being part of the Savage Brotherhood means you have to do hard things. Is that what you want?"

Stewart felt his anger draining away. He turned his face. After what he had seen and done, did he still want to be part of this? *Yes. To stop something like this happening again.*

He took in a deep breath. "I will be an alpha someday. Sooner, rather than later."

Typhoon’s lips twitched.

“And in the meantime, what happens to me? I killed vampires in vampire territory. The treaty...”

This time, Typhoon all-out grinned. “Ah. Well, you see that’s another reason I chose you for this mission. You’re under Guinevere's protection. By vampire law, as her brother-in-law, you’re her citizen. The rules aren’t quite the same for you. There will be no repercussions against you or Frieda... so long as you marry within an appropriate timeframe.”

Stewart stared at him, trying to figure out if he was telling the truth or not. There was no joke in Typhoon’s eyes. Stewart snorted. Sure. He’d get right on that... but he couldn’t stop himself from smiling at the thought of

Frieda dressed all in white. He would get right on that indeed!

# Chapter Twelve

*Polaris*

A month after the assassination of Rudolph, things more or less calmed down. Guinevere officially annexed the kingdom, making Frieda and Stewart's actions somewhat legal in the eyes of vampire law. She wasn't exactly thrilled about the added responsibility, but Twister assured Frieda that she wasn't going to back out of it.

Frieda was no longer afraid of a flare-up of vampire venom, either. She had never recovered so fast before, and that was thanks to Dr. Mia. The tiger shifter really did have a way with medicine. It was a relief to be discharged from Guinevere's personal hospital. The scent of vampire was really starting to grate on her, even if she did have plenty of shifter visitors during the day.

Perhaps one of the greatest things to come out of the whole assassination debacle was that Twister had finally calmed down about her relationship with Stewart. *"It's not that I didn't want you two together,"* he had explained to her while driving her back to her place once she was discharged. *"It was more that it was just weird... like finding my sister and brother... you know. I never knew you felt that way toward him. Honestly, part of it was because I was miffed at the two of you for not telling me."*

Frieda smirked as she glanced over to her left, where Stewart sat in a tattoo chair. She lay on her stomach, naked to the waist, while her tattoo artist worked on the new tat she had designed for this occasion. Stewart grinned at her as his artist finished up the detail of the wolf's head on his arm.

He was officially a member of the Savage Brotherhood now. Typhoon had had a ceremony and everything. At the ceremony, Stewart had pulled out an old ring he'd gotten from a pawn shop—legally—and got to one knee before her. When he asked her to marry him, there had been no other answer than yes.

Stewart would be getting a rose to match hers on their next visit. And in a year or two, they would be married. Frieda would have preferred to elope right away, but Roxy had flat-out threatened to kill her if she stole her littlest brother's wedding away from her, so Frieda had relented to the big white wedding.

Her mate and fiancé cast an appreciative glance down her body, and she gave him the same look right back. He'd changed, physically, since he became a shifter. While he had always been tall and strong, there was a fine-tuning of his muscular frame that was subtle yet made a huge difference. Or maybe it was just that he held himself with more confidence now.

In any case, it was all she could do not to throw herself at him right then, in front of everybody.

His artist wiped up the bit of blood from around the tattoo and started the final process of covering it for the duration of healing. It'd be perfectly fine by the time they got back to her place, but the artists didn't know that.

Stewart inspected her new tat as her artist finishcd up as well. “It suits you. All the colors of the northern lights in a rose. Beautiful. Elegant. Just like you.”

Frieda couldn’t help but blush at that. It seemed a little ridiculous to her that she got so embarrassed by the smallest of things these days, but only when it came to Stewart. She had never had a real relationship before... not like this. Of course, she was prone to thinking that nobody had ever had a relationship like this before. It was the most wonderful thing she had ever experienced...

When her tattoo was done, they jumped onto her bike and headed to her place. She loved the feeling of his arms around her waist as she dodged through traffic, getting a special thrill every time some idiot thought she was hogging the road and purposefully got too close—only for her to leave them in the dust. Stewart's hot breath was on the back of her neck, making her core tighten and her skin tingle. She already knew exactly what she wanted to do with him once they were back at her place.

Stewart had more or less moved in with her. It hadn't been something that they'd really talked about so much as it just sort of happened. Between their need for privacy and Daniel now living at Stewart's apartment, the alternatives were alleys, hotels or just out in the forest. Admittedly, they had done that a few times—and once were almost caught by Brad Duster, who still seemed to have it out for her. Not that she cared as much these days. He kept his distance with the important things and just seemed to have a personal grudge against her. She was going to invite him to the wedding just for kicks.

Once they got to her apartment, a shoebox of a bachelor's suite above the subways, Frieda peeled the bandage off Stewart's arm and started to dab on a moisturizer.

"You know, I always knew you'd be a member of the Brotherhood one day," she mused aloud. "Even before you were a shifter. I knew somehow you'd get yourself initiated. It was only a matter of time. Typhoon wouldn't be able to keep you out."

Stewart snorted. "Even if I never became a shifter?"

"Hell yeah. You are nothing if not a determined bastard."

Stewart took her hand in his, stilling it. When she met his gaze, her breath was taken away at the depth of emotion in his eyes. “The cost was almost too great.”

Frieda flushed slightly as she shrugged and looked away. “It really wasn’t that bad, Stewart. I’ve been bitten before. I’ve always pulled through, even without the venom being sucked away.”

Stewart shook his head. Some emotion flashed deep in his eyes as his hand tightened around hers. “That’s not what I meant, Frieda. And I think you know that.”

She did know that. And she knew why there was that haunted look in his eyes, too. They hadn’t talked about what Rudolph had wanted from her, what he had very nearly taken from her. She had dreams about it, woke up sometimes drenched in sweat. She knew it was going to be something that would take time to get over.

"But it didn't happen," she whispered to him. She cupped his face in her hands and he kissed her palm. "You saved me. In more ways than one. I know it was terrifying for you, too. But I'm fine. You're fine. And I love you."

Stewart kissed her lightly, then rested his forehead against hers. "I love you, too. Have for a very long time."

Frieda smirked. "Oh, I know. And it was only a matter of time before I gave in to your charms. You were my perfect mate from the moment we met, even if I was too afraid to see that at first."

He pressed another kiss to her lips, a little harder this time. “You? Afraid? Perish the thought.”

“Mmmm…” Frieda wrapped her arms around his neck. She pulled him in for a deeper, longer kiss, a smile starting to curl her lips. This was what she wanted, everything she needed. And she wanted to share everything with Stewart another time.

Frieda flicked her fingers over the buttons on his shirt, opening them one by one until his muscled, tattooed chest was bare to her. Then she moved down from his mouth, her lips coasting over his throat until she tasted the words written above his heart. Stewart reached out and tugged up her tank, tossing it aside before he pushed her jeans down off her hips.

"I believe you promised me somcthing last time," he told her, eyes sparkling, when he looked up at her again.

Frieda arched a brow. She didn't remember promising anything the previous night...

"You were going to scream my name."

Oh. She remembered now. Heat flooded her body at the look in Stewart's eyes. She opened her mouth to make a witty comeback, but he seized her around the waist, and the next thing she knew, she was on the floor with his hot, huge body caging her. Somehow, he'd managed to tear off her clothes even as he laid her down, and his hands made fireworks explode under her skin as they roved over her body.

His hot, wet mouth came to her breasts, sucking one nipple into a hard point before moving to the other. Something snapped deep inside of her, pulling so tight that she had to let out a moan. Her head pressed into the floor as she arched her body, trying to get him even closer. She reached between them, finding his still-clothed cock and massaged him through his jeans.

Stewart groaned, moving back to her mouth. His hand pushed between her thighs and found her clit, playing around it with a deft touch that had her moaning with need. His tongue thrust into her mouth, and she found herself unable to keep up her ministrations on him. She gasped, clutching her hands around his face as his hand still played with her clit, while the other shifted her thigh up to his hip. The rough fabric of his jeans rasped against her leg as she gasped again.

Heat flooded through her body, reaching to her fingertips and all the way to her toes. Her core tightened with need and she rocked her hips, trying to increase the pressure on her clit. Stewart chuckled as he delved into her neck. Her skin burned with desire as his free hand continued to roam. When he snapped open his jeans, she had to gasp yet another time—he sprang free of the fabric and pressed hard against her leg.

"Stewart," she whispered, moving her hands to his arms to ensure she didn't mark him up. The skin at his tattoo was still a little warmer than the rest of him, and she traced it with a single finger.

“Frieda,” he whispered back, then slid a finger inside of her.

“Oh! Gods that’s good,” she sighed as he curled his finger, stroking her insides while working her clit with his thumb.

Somehow, she managed to reach down again and take his cock in her hand. At first, her hand tightened in uncontrollable spasms, in time with his strokes to her clit. Stewart hissed and eased off, allowing her to stroke him in more controlled motions. They pleasured each other for some time while sweat dewed on their bodies and their limbs trembled with desire and exertion.

“I love you,” Stewart whispered again. His eyes were at half-mast, that look of exquisite torture on his face.

Frieda knew better than to expect more words from him now; he was too deep in pleasure, too concentrated on holding off his orgasm so she could finish first. So she moved her hands to his and guided him into position. He entered her smoothly, her wetness already at its peak. He filled her perfectly, as he always did.

She clutched at his arms as he started to thrust. She couldn't remember the last time she'd let herself be topped so often; surely never by one man like this before. She stared into his eyes as pleasure flooded her body, her heart pounding and her hands tightening on his arms. His head dropped, kissing her again and again and again. She tried to keep up with all the kisses but couldn't. Eventually, he had to move down to her neck, and from there his back bent, hips still pumping rhythmically, as he returned to her breasts. Her whole body felt like it was on fire. She couldn't breathe. Her arms and legs trembled as shivers of pleasure moved up and down her spine.

Her orgasm took her all at once. Waves of darkness washed over her vision, her back arched and she was screaming. Whether his name or not, she couldn't really tell. Stewart gasped in relief. His motions became jerky and he finished into her with a series of grunts and groans before they both fell back, utterly spent.

It was several minutes before either of them had the brain power or breath to speak again. When they did, they murmured that they loved each other before rolling to their sides, still joined together, until they slowly drifted off to sleep. Frieda snuggled in her lover's arms, warm and safe and feeling utterly content.

"Love you," she murmured sleepily.

Stewart touched the bandages on her back that covered up her new tattoo. "Love you, too."

*****

THE END

16263272R00146

Printed in Great Britain
by Amazon